THE
GRAVE
DIGGER

THE GRAVE DIGGER

Rebecca Bischoff

Illustrations by Tambe

AMBERJACK
PUBLISHING

IDAHO

Amberjack Publishing
1472 E. Iron Eagle Drive
Eagle, ID 83616
http://amberjackpublishing.com

Copyright © 2019 by Rebecca Bischoff

10 9 8 7 6 5 4 3 2 1

Library of Congress Cataloging-in-Publication Data
Names: Bischoff, Rebecca, author. | Tambellini, Stefano, illustrator.
Title: The grave digger / Rebecca Bischoff.
Description: Idaho : Amberjack Publishing, 2019.
Identifiers: LCCN 2019017846 (print) | LCCN 2019020960 (ebook) | ISBN
   9781948705530 (ebook) | ISBN 9781948705523 (hardback)
Subjects: | CYAC: Grave robbing--Fiction. | Dead--Fiction. | Medical
   care--History--19th century--Fiction. | Race relations--Fiction. | Family
   life--Ohio--Fiction. | Ohio--History--19th century--Fiction. | Horror
   stories. | BISAC: JUVENILE FICTION / Mysteries & Detective Stories. |
   JUVENILE FICTION / Horror & Ghost Stories.
Classification: LCC PZ7.1.B5463 (ebook) | LCC PZ7.1.B5463 Gr 2019 (print) |
   DDC [Fic]--dc23
LC record available at https://lccn.loc.gov/2019017846

ISBN: 978-1-948705-52-3
E-ISBN: 978-1-948705-53-0

For my mother, Evelyn Israel,
who taught me to love books.

ONE

NOVEMBER 1875

CIRCLEVILLE, OHIO

R AISING THE DEAD was hard work.

Cap had been warned of it. He thought he was ready. He'd expected backbreaking, soul-wearying, and bone-chilling drudgery, but not this. Here he was, underground, surrounded by dark and dirt while a corpse lay inches away. His hands ached with a fierce cold and his body trembled so that he could hardly control his limbs.

Hard work didn't begin to describe it.

"Hurry, boy," hissed an ugly voice from the entrance of the black tunnel. Columbus Jones, or "Lum," as he called himself. Cap's stomach clenched itself into a cold ball. The man must have poked his fat head into the hole, and his words stabbed through the darkness.

"He's taking too long," Lum said. "The trumpets'll sound and the dead will all awake afore that boy finishes his job."

A moment later, the distinctive voice of Cap's father, Noah, murmured in response.

"He'll do it," Father said. "You'll see."

But worry and doubt colored the man's words like a tune played on the wrong piano keys. That, more than anything, spurred the boy onward.

He reached out and felt the cool, splintery wood with trembling fingers, found the head of a nail and pried it loose with his hammer. Despite the chill, a drop of sweat rolled down the side of his forehead as he tore away more nails one by one. And the easy part was done.

Cap removed the head of the coffin and slid it behind him. Then, he seized the thick rope he'd dragged along. Now came the real test. He stretched trembling fingers in front of him. After an eternal moment, his fingertips touched a head of springy hair.

"Mother of God!" he blurted as he wrenched his hand away. The cold ham he'd had for supper began to squeal and work its way back out of his belly. Cap scrabbled backward.

I can't do it, he thought, shaking his head. *No sirree!*

"Cap?" Father called. "Ready, son?"

The man's voice was strained. Father needed him.

Fighting the violent tremors that shook him all over, Cap brought the rope forward. He worked it around the head and shoulders of the unresisting body and then moved it under the arms. The flesh of the corpse was soft, its limbs easy to shift. For all he knew, this person could simply be asleep. Thick braids tangled in the boy's fingers.

It was a woman. Cap couldn't help picturing his mother, home in bed and sick with fever. Mamma was swollen with another child who would probably be born too soon, like the others. And she plaited her hair when she went to bed.

"We need the money," Cap whispered. Over and over, he repeated the words. Mamma wasn't well. They did indeed need all the coin they could get.

With renewed strength, Cap knotted the rope and gave the signal, a sharp whistle. Grunting softly, the men outside the tunnel pulled on their end of the rope. Inch by inch, the woman slipped out of her eternal rest, eased through the tunnel, and finally emerged above ground.

Scrambling out after her, Cap stood and stretched stiff legs, gulping crisp air that smelled of rotting leaves. He gazed up at a patch of stars that sparkled through a tiny gap in the clouds. The pinpoints of light, like a scattering of diamond dust in the sky, made a comforting sight.

"Help us, boy!" Lum hissed. "Don't stand there lollygagging up at them stars. This job ain't over, yet!"

Blinking, Cap stumbled over to assist his father and Lum as they lifted the slight form into the back of the waiting wagon. Lum's shuttered lantern was open only a fraction of an inch. It gave a thin beam of golden light that barely pierced the ocean of black ink around them.

"What did I tell you?" Father said. Then, the man's hand fell upon his son's shoulder, and the surrounding darkness seemed lighter.

"I'll allow you that, Noah," Lum admitted, chuckling. He slapped Cap on the back so hard the boy stumbled. "Didn't think your boy had the grit."

"Cap may be knee high to a milk stool, but he's as full of grit as any boy twice his size," Father said, his words now certain. "And he's near to reaching his thirteenth year. He'll be a man, soon."

At those words, Cap unconsciously stretched himself, trying to look taller.

The men began to scrape dirt back into the tunnel. "Back to work, boy!" Lum barked. "You'll make a poor fist of this business with your lazy-dog ways."

With fingers aching from the cold, Cap seized another shovel and began to heave clods of earth into the hole, while his thoughts roiled in his head. Father had warned him to obey Lum's orders and keep his trap shut, but words sprouted from the boy's lips before he could stop them.

"This tunnel was a fool idea!" he blurted, shoveling dirt as fast as he could into the hole. "It'll take us an hour to fill it in. We should've just dug through the dirt right above the grave. It's still soft from when they made the hole this morning."

"All right, then, you smart-mouthed little cur," Lum hissed. He grabbed Cap's arm and steered him back to the wagon. "If you don't like your job, you take the clothes off! We gotta leave them or we're stealing, remember?"

Father hurried over. "I'll do that," he said. "My boy will finish filling the tunnel."

With a wheezing chuckle, Lum dropped Cap's arm and the boy returned to his shovel, his shoulders sagging with relief. He'd forgotten one detail: The law said it was illegal to steal *from* the dead. You couldn't take jewelry or anything buried with them, including their clothing. The law said nothing about stealing the dead themselves. They weren't anybody's property.

"Who's there?" a man shouted. The sudden sound pierced the cold night air.

Cap dropped his shovel and whirled. Light glowed in the distance, and the cemetery gate clanged open.

"Run, boy!" Lum said. "Your pa and I'll take care of the goods. You scat; you'll slow us down."

Without hesitation, Cap darted into the trees at the far edge of Forest Cemetery and flew across fields lying bleak in the cold November air. Shouts grew fainter by the moment. His breath came out in harsh gasps and his chest and legs ached something fierce. Still he ran, stumbling over frozen furrows and clattering across the wooden footbridge that crossed the stream and led to his streets.

Finally, the welcoming shape of his home loomed ahead. Cap squeezed through the gap in the fence. With a heart clattering like horses' hooves on a cobbled street, he hurried to the old willow tree. The hanging branches, bare and brittle, parted with thin whispers as he slithered through them. Reaching the well-hidden door that led to his workshop, he slipped inside.

Cap plopped down onto the stool beside his worktable and struggled to breathe. Then he dropped his head onto his folded arms, near to worn out.

If his work ended up like this, night after night, raising the dead was going to kill him.

TWO

"WAKE UP, CAP," Mamma said.

The boy bolted upright, squinting in the morning light. He'd spent the night hunched over his worktable. He glanced at his mother, half-expecting her to be livid or frantic; but Mamma was smiling.

"I almost regret letting Noah build this shop for you," she said. She placed a plate of fluffy biscuits spread with strawberry jam on the table at Cap's elbow. "It's bad enough you spend every waking minute here. Now I even find you curled up to sleep beside your precious tools!" Mamma chuckled and ruffled Cap's honey-colored hair. His mother's words, spoken in her refined English accent, were gentle. Cap breathed out a sigh of relief.

"Why, Cap, is that your warming box?" she asked, pointing to a wooden box in the corner.

"Yes, ma'am." He'd built it recently as a home for newly hatched chicks. A thin sheet of metal served as the base, and below that was a space to hold hot-water bottles to heat the base and warm the inside of the box.

"What a clever idea," Mamma said. "That should save some of our chickens come spring."

She rubbed her ever-growing belly, while her breath puffed out into the cold air of the workshop in tiny white clouds. Mamma's usually rosy face was nearly light as cream, while bluish-gray smudges were apparent under her eyes.

"Are you well, Mamma?" Cap asked.

"Well enough, thank you. A bit more tired than usual, but Dr. Ivins will be by this morning. Oh, I do hope Noah was able to…" her voice trailed off.

Able to scrape together enough money to pay the doctor. Cap spoke in his head the words Mamma didn't say aloud. But where was Father? Had he and Lum gotten caught?

"Bring your plate to the kitchen when you're done," Mamma said, moving to the door. "And wash up before you head to school. You look like you rolled in a pigsty last night."

With a start, Cap began to slap at the dried dirt that coated his jacket and trousers. Father would whip him but good if he ever let slip the truth of what the men of the family had started to do on dark nights.

Cleaning accomplished, Cap tucked into his hot biscuits. He licked melted butter and sweet jam off his thumb and scolded himself for falling asleep at his worktable. Finishing quickly, he rose and headed to the washroom to scrub his face and hands.

Somewhat cleaner in appearance, he hurried downstairs. Mrs. Hardy, their elderly housekeeper, plucked the plate from his hands and shooed him toward the front door.

"March, young man," she said. But suddenly, she grabbed his shoulders while her narrowed green eyes traveled over Cap's rumpled clothing.

"Look at the state o' you," the gray-haired woman said, clucking her tongue. The creases about the woman's eyes crinkled even more deeply. "If I didn't know any better, I'd say you spent the night sleeping in the dirt." Mrs. Hardy's Irish brogue colored her words more than usual whenever she scolded him.

Cap stifled a laugh, but then grimaced as Mrs. Hardy began to brush the dirt from his jacket with strength surprising for a woman her age.

"What would Mina say if she saw you like this? Your mother raised you better, Cap." Finished with her cleaning, the house-keeper took the boy once more by the shoulders. "So did I," she added. Her eyes twinkled. "Now go," Mrs. Hardy said, opening the door wide and pushing him gently through. "Godspeed. Don't be late." She tweaked one of his ears, as she did each morning, turned in a whirl of blue gingham, and closed the door behind her with a solid thud.

Hunched against the cold, Cap plodded across his front yard to the gate. He arrived just in time to open it for the woman who stood on the other side, bundled in a thick coat and carrying a heavy basket. It was Jardine Cole, Dr. Ivins's brown-skinned as-sistant, who sometimes came along to help tend the patients.

Lately, she'd begun to come here on her own, leaving something for Mamma each time she did: small packets of herbs or cakes dotted with raisins. In return, she often borrowed one of Mamma's many books.

"Good morning," she said. Her large brown eyes, ringed with long lashes, were friendly.

Cap nodded a greeting, while out on the street, Dr. Ivins was climbing down from his carriage. The tall man smoothed his chestnut-brown hair that was tied back with a ribbon at the nape of his neck. He straightened his vest and brushed at a speck on his crumpled coat.

"Hello, Cap," he said with a weary smile. "How is our bright young inventor this morning? Anything new?"

Scuffing his boot in the dirt, Cap grinned and explained his warming box project.

"That sounds promising," Dr. Ivins said, making Cap beam. "And how is your mamma this morning?" The man was usually clean shaven, but today a scattering of dark whiskers on his cheeks made his already pale complexion seem even lighter.

"Well enough, sir," Cap said. As the doctor approached the gate, the man stifled a yawn.

"Our poor doctor can hardly leave the hospital," Jardine told Cap. "I believe he's slept there for days."

"One must do what one must do," Dr. Ivins said, covering another yawn. "Many people are getting sick. Two died this morning."

"Died?" Cap blurted. Dr. Ivins nodded solemnly. A jolt of fear hit Cap in the stomach. Why, he'd be right back at the cemetery before two shakes of a lamb's tail.

"That's too bad," he managed to say, closing the latch behind him. Before he took another step, a plump woman wrapped in a threadbare shawl hurried from a house down the street, calling and waving. She reached them and handed a basket full of eggs to Dr. Ivins, practically shoving them into his arms.

"For curing my wee Lisbeth," she said. The tiny woman stretched up on her toes to plant a kiss on the doctor's cheek before scurrying back to her house.

Jardine chuckled as the doctor turned pink as a summer rose. "Why, that's real nice," she said with a dimpled smile.

Dr. Ivins cleared his throat but said nothing.

"Well, I'd best hurry. The school bell's about to ring," Cap said.

Jardine and Dr. Ivins waved to him and turned toward the house, while Cap trotted down the street.

A small knot of boys from his neighborhood were at the end of the block. A ginger-haired boy with a face like a speckled hen's egg caught Cap's eye. He turned and said something to the others, and they burst into laughter. Then, they broke into a run, turned the corner, and disappeared.

Wonder what those fellows would say if they knew what I got myself up to last night? Cap thought.

A broad smile sprouted on his face. Then just as quickly, it wilted like a dying flower and faded away. They'd almost been caught. What would have happened if they had been?

THREE

B REAKING INTO A trot, Cap made it to school just as Master
Rankin rang the bell a final time. Everyone else was already
seated in his classroom. All eyes turned to him as he entered.
Scowling, he hurried to his desk.

"How grand of you to join us," Master Rankin told him with a
wintry smile.

Cap's face burned.

The boy spent the morning fighting to stay awake but often lost
the battle. When Master Rankin rang the bell for the midday
break, Cap yawned and wearily rose from his seat.

"You look mighty tired," a girl said. Cap glanced up at a pair of
sparkling black eyes. They belonged to Jessamyn, the girl who sat
in front of him. Every so often, he was tempted to reach out and

tug the thick braid that always hung down her back. Gently, of course.

He froze. Jessamyn hardly ever spoke to him, or to anyone else, for that matter. He opened his mouth but nothing came out. The girl's eyes weren't black like he'd first thought. They were a deep brown, the color of chestnuts in the fall.

Jessamyn smiled. "Oh, I don't mean to tease," she said. "I only wanted to let you know that your slate pencil rolled under my desk. Here it is." She held it out.

Their fingers brushed when Cap took the pencil, and a warmth spread through him.

"Thanks," he said.

The girl smiled again, and a flush brightened her fair golden skin. She reached beneath her chair for her lunch pail and turned away. Cap followed her with his eyes as she went to join the small group gathering near the oil stove.

"Ain't you never seen a girl before?" someone said. Cap scowled up at the talker. It was Eli, the red-headed boy who'd said something to make the other boys laugh at him earlier that morning.

"'Course I have," he said. He hurriedly lifted the top of his desk to stuff his slate and pencil inside. He let the lid of the desk slam into place with a loud clatter.

"Must you be so rough with the school's property, Mr. Cooper?" Master Rankin said as he approached. He paused and dropped a folded newspaper on one of the desks. Then, he pulled a handkerchief from his pocket and dabbed at his nose.

Eli leaned close to Cap and whispered: "I know why you like *her*."

Cap squinted at him. "What the devil do you mean by that?"

But Eli just smirked and walked away, whistling. Shaking his head, Cap turned toward the door but stopped short at the sight of the headline on Master Rankin's paper:

Ghoulish Robbers Steal a Stiff from Forest Cemetery.
Will Your Loved One Be Next?

He gasped.

Master Rankin picked up the paper and quickly tucked it under his arm. "It is terrible, isn't it?" he said.

Cap said nothing.

The schoolteacher sighed loudly as he folded his handkerchief and put it away. Then he glanced down at Cap with a smile much friendlier than his usual cold sneer. "You'd best hurry home for your meal. See that you return on time."

Cap turned and bolted from the room, leaping down the school steps and sprinting toward the center of town. He was hungry, but food was the last thing on his mind.

In town, he made a quick check of the dustbins behind the grocer's but came up empty. No one had tossed away any newspapers. Cap left the alleyway and hustled around the corner, where he promptly collided into someone. Books and papers scattered, and a young woman whose hair was wrapped in a blue scarf gaped at him.

"I'm sorry," he said, gasping for breath. He bent down to retrieve a fallen book that was so thick he had to lift it with two hands. "This sure is heavy," he added, straightening and holding it out.

He blinked in surprise. The older girl's face, with its brown skin and eyes ringed with thick lashes, was the younger image of the woman he'd spoken to that morning.

"Why, you look just like Jardine!"

The girl's eyebrows flew skyward. "How do you know my mother?" she asked. She straightened and took the book he offered.

"I've met her. She works for Dr. Ivins and visits Mamma sometimes."

"That's right," the girl said, her face alight. "I work with Dr. Ivins, too, you know," she added, brushing off her green skirt. "I'm going to be a doctor myself one day. My name is Philadelphia." She held out her hand to the boy.

"You're going to be a doctor?" Cap asked. "But you're a…" He gulped and paused, with the jolting realization that he'd spoken without thought.

The girl dropped her hand, while heat rushed to Cap's face.

"I'm a what?" she asked. A crinkle appeared between her arched brows.

"You're a girl," Cap said, reaching up to loosen his scarf, which suddenly felt tight about his neck. "Girls aren't doctors."

Philadelphia threw her head back and laughed out loud, while curious onlookers glanced at the two as they hurried past in the cold.

Cap gawked at her. Why in blazes did she think that was funny?

"Oh, my goodness," Philadelphia said, once she'd caught her breath. She dabbed at her glistening eyes with the corner of her coat sleeve. "Why, I surely did need that laugh. Thank you."

Blinking, Cap muttered, "Uh, you're welcome?"

The older girl chuckled again. Balancing her heavy parcel of books on her hip, she smiled down at him.

"I could have sworn you were going to say I was a colored girl," she told him, shaking her head. "Well, I did enjoy the laugh you just gave me. You see, after the news this morning, I'm all in a dither." Her face grew serious. "You've heard, haven't you?"

The red knit scarf about Cap's neck seemed to tighten again of its own accord. He nodded.

"I can't quite believe what the paper said about why they think that poor woman was dug up. Who would have thought this could happen in our little town? Oh, never you mind," Philadelphia said, glancing down at Cap and smiling once more. "Thank you again for making me laugh."

"Glad I could help," he mumbled.

Philadelphia grinned. "Well, you best remember this: Girls most certainly can be doctors, and this girl is going to be the best doctor our town's ever seen," she said, lifting her chin. "By the way, what's your name?" she added, as she began to move slowly down the sidewalk.

"I'm Captain," he answered. "Captain Cooper." He followed along while trying to gather his thoughts.

"I want to tell you something, Captain," Philadelphia said as they walked. "Last week I attended an anatomy lecture at the hospital. You know what anatomy is?" she asked.

Gulping, Cap studied his worn boots as they walked. "'Course I do," he said. "The study of the human body."

"It was a lecture all about the inside workings of our bodies. The doctors showed us wonderful drawings. One was of the heart and lungs, and another was a complete drawing of a skeleton. One showed the brain and what it looks like when it's cut open." She glanced at Cap with a mischievous gleam in her eyes.

He couldn't meet her gaze.

"Why, Captain, does that frighten you? You look a might sick," the girl said in a teasing tone. "One fellow, a sass-mouthed man all slicked up in his Sunday best, he told me I should leave. 'Course, I didn't. And I bet he was sure sorry he said anything. Least ways," Philadelphia said, leaning closer as though to share a secret, "I'm certain he was powerfully sorry when he couldn't answer any of the questions those doctors asked us, while I knew the answer to every single one."

Despite the chill that had seeped into his heart after reading the morning's headline, Cap laughed.

Philadelphia beamed at him. "Girls can surely be doctors," she told him again. "We've been healers for ages and ages. We're made of tougher stuff than you think, Captain."

"Call me Cap," the boy said. "The only person who calls me Captain is my mamma."

The girl reached her hand out once more and this time gave Cap a firm handshake.

"Call me Delphia," she said, while her lips curled with mirth. "The only person who calls me Philadelphia is my mamma."

With that, she turned to enter the nearby red-brick building. "I'm off to study at the library. Nice to meet you, Cap."

"Likewise," Cap said, watching her disappear through the doorway.

When he turned to go, his brief amusement faded as fast as the sun on a winter evening. Biting his lip, he returned to his search for a newspaper. Delphia Cole was sure all-fired determined to be a doctor, but did she know what would happen when she got to medical college?

Cap filled his cheeks and blew out his breath in a long, white stream. Father had explained that medical schools bought the bodies they dug up, cutting them apart in front of their students. "Doctors need to know how we're put together and how everything works," he'd said.

Shaking his head, the boy hurried down the street. Did Delphia know about that?

FOUR

CAP HURRIED TO his next stop, the shop of the local watch-maker, Mr. Garrett. His stomach growled. Dinner hour was nearly over, but he wasn't ready to admit defeat and return to school. If he couldn't find a free paper, well, he'd have to earn a few coins and buy one.

From the time Cap was small, he'd been fascinated by the whirring gears inside a timepiece and had spent countless hours with his nose pressed to the glass of the shop. Two summers be-fore, Mr. Garrett invited him inside to see how a clock worked. Cap was in awe, and the two became fast friends, especially since the boy was a quick learner. Now, Mr. Garrett was glad to have nimble fingers and young eyes to help him with the delicate work that had become more difficult of late.

"Cap!" Mr. Garrett said as he swung the door open. The magnifying glass the man used when repairing timepieces was attached to the frames of his spectacles, making one watery blue eye enormous. His steel-gray hair stood on end, and he walked with a limp thanks to an old injury. Cap always thought Mr. Garrett looked part human and part wind-up toy.

"Do you have any work for me, Mr. Garrett?" he asked. "Something small, seeing as it's my dinner hour and I need to get back to school soon."

"Matter of fact, I do," the man said, pivoting to hobble off toward the workroom behind the shop front. "Come on in."

Though he was in a hurry, Cap paused to admire his favorite timepiece: a fancy cuckoo clock that ticked away in a steady beat. As each new hour was announced, not only did a tiny bird pop out to tell the time, but carved and painted figures danced in a circle while a waterwheel turned around and around. A real trickle of water flowed into a tiny pond.

Mr. Garrett's daughter, Lettie, waved a greeting to Cap as he passed. "That came all the way from Germany, you know," she told him. Strands of the young woman's long, yellow hair hung in her face as she turned back to her ledger and frowned at the rows of scribbled numbers.

"You added wrong again, Papa," she called.

"Bother," was all Mr. Garrett said. He led Cap to his workroom, where broken clocks, watches, and automated toys sat in a jumble on a long table, waiting to be repaired. In the corner was a large wooden crate marked "Fresh Pickles." Sitting on top of the crate was a coil of wire and a small metal box that had bits of wire sticking out in several places.

"Special order," Mr. Garrett said, nodding toward the pickle crate. "Been working on that all week."

"What is it?" Cap asked.

"Some contraption a man asked me to design. Don't know how well it'll work yet, but we'll see."

Cap worked quickly as he could, piecing together a pocket watch while Mr. Garrett supervised. The old watchmaker chatted about this and that while he worked, never expecting a reply. Tension melted from his shoulders as Cap concentrated on his task. But then, Mr. Garrett's next words stole his breath.

"You hear o' that business at the cemetery?" the old man asked. Cap nearly dropped the tweezers he'd been using to put a tiny cog in place.

"Knew her, I did. Nellie. Nice old gal. Sharp tongue, but a good soul, for one o' them."

Cap opened his mouth to speak the question that trembled on the tip of his tongue, but then he pressed his lips together. He already knew what *one of them* meant. He hadn't gotten a good look at the body…at *Nellie*, after they'd swiped her from the ground, being it was so dark and all. But he *had* felt her thick, wiry braids. Nellie must have been one of the town's colored residents, like Delphia, and her mother, Jardine.

Swallowing hard, he used the special tiny hammer to tap the round metal backing into place on the pocket watch. When he carefully wound the timepiece, it began to tick a solid, slow, steady beat.

"Done," he said.

"Good boy," Mr. Garrett said, patting Cap on the shoulder. "Fine work as usual."

Cap took the offered coins without looking at them and shoved them into his pocket, slinging his jacket about his shoulders. After waving goodbye, he hurried toward the market to buy a paper. He read the story on the way back to school, hardly minding where he put his feet.

Ghoulish Robbers Steal a Stiff from Forest Cemetery. Will Your Loved One Be Next?

Elizabeth Jackson, known as "Nellie," aged sixty-four, was unlawfully removed from her final resting place last night in Forest Cemetery, shocking our little community.

"My Nellie's grave was empty," said her husband, Mr. Wilford Jackson, aged sixty-seven. "What'd somebody go and dig her up for?"

The answer to that may lie in the nearby city of Columbus, says Dr. Alfred Winthrop, a retired medical man. "Medical students must have fresh cadavers to pass their anatomy courses," he told the paper. "Grave robbing is unfortunately common near cities where there are medical schools."

Inquiries were sent early this morning by telegraph to Starling Medical College in Columbus. We await a response. Our lawmen have no leads as to who may have committed this gruesome crime. Mr. Jackson asks the townspeople to keep a watchful eye out for any clues as to the whereabouts of his wife's remains.

"She ain't there no more. Where am I supposed to leave the flowers?" Mr. Jackson told the paper.

Scowling, Cap folded the paper and trotted back toward the brick school building. He'd missed his midday meal, but there was nothing to do about it now. His thoughts weren't really on food, anyway. There had to be some *other* way for Father to earn extra money. Something that didn't involve stealing folks from their graves.

"You never said you wouldn't be here for your dinner today," the housekeeper said with a sniff when Cap entered the kitchen after school.

"I had to stay and do my history essay," he replied. A jab of guilt over his lie poked somewhere around the vicinity of his stomach.

Mrs. Hardy's eyebrows raised. "You mean to say you've eaten nothing since breakfast?"

At the boy's nod, the housekeeper sighed. "Well, supper's ready, so we'll make an early meal of it. Your mamma's feeling poorly again." Her face was flushed pink from the heat of the stove. She swept strands of silver hair behind her ears as she plunked a full plate down onto the red tablecloth. "She'll eat in her room later. Your father won't be home yet, so it's the two of us. Say grace," she added, nodding sternly at the boy. "And remove your cap, young man."

Doing as he was told, Cap bowed his head and mumbled a swift prayer, thanking God for the food.

"Louder next time," Mrs. Hardy said, pouring him a cup of milk. "Perhaps God heard you, but I didn't."

"*I* heard you, plain as day," Father said, as he threw open the kitchen door and flung his coat over a chair. "And next time you want to pray to the Old Man, tell him we're tired of this bloody foul weather. That we can do without."

Mrs. Hardy gasped as she did whenever Father used what she called "rough language."

"Now, really, Mr. Cooper," she began, but Father cut her off.

"Aw, now, don't scold me and say I'm not to speak so in front of the boy," he said with a wide grin, taking the plate the scandalized housekeeper handed to him. He tucked into his potatoes with gusto. "This weather *is* bloody foul, wouldn't you say, Cap?"

Cap snorted out a laugh. Mrs. Hardy threw her hands into the air and looked heavenward with a sigh before turning back to her bubbling pots. Her cheeks now bore twin spots of bright red, but she was grinning.

"Heathen," she muttered with a chuckle.

"Old wet hen," Father replied, dunking his bread into his milk and popping the sodden bite into his mouth.

"Old *Irish* hen, thank you very much," Mrs. Hardy said.

Father barked out a laugh.

Suddenly sober, Cap wolfed his food. He was itching to know what had happened after he'd fled the cemetery, but he and Father couldn't exactly discuss their "business" in front of Mrs. Hardy. He tried nudging Father once, but the man ignored him. With a shrug, Cap jammed half a piece of apple pie into his mouth, mumbled an excuse, and hurried off to his room.

His mattress was stuffed with straw, but to Cap it was soft as downy feathers. He was just about to sink into much-needed sleep when a tap on his door woke him.

"Mm?" he mumbled.

Father opened the door and crossed the room.

"Thought I'd let you know that Lum delivered the goods. We'll have our payment soon."

"Oh," Cap said. He propped himself up on one elbow. "How did you get away?"

Father chuckled. "I drove the wagon through the hedge. We hid in the woods until all was clear. Then Lum took off on foot to make the delivery."

"Where does Lum take the, uh, you know." Cap cleared his throat. "*Them*?" he asked.

Father's shoulders stiffened, and he faced his son. "I don't know, Cap. We're hired to dig them up, and that's what we do. We don't ask questions."

"But Father—"

Father placed a finger to his lips. "I brought you into this business because I need help. Keep quiet and do as you're told. We need this job." He closed his eyes. "We need the money, son."

"Yes, sir," Cap whispered. "But we were nearly found out. It's in the paper."

"I know," Father said. He paused with his hand on the doorknob. "We'll lay low for a week or so, but talk'll die down. Besides, we only take the ones who won't be missed. Get some rest." The door closed behind him with a soft click.

Rest didn't come easy. Cap tossed about as though his bed were made of rusted nails and horseshoes. Nellie *was* missed. Someone wanted to put flowers on her grave.

FIVE

J ESSAMYN WASN'T IN school the next day or the day after, which was Friday. Cap didn't truly mind. Eli had no chance to taunt him about her.

When the weekend finally came, Cap spent most of Saturday tinkering in his shop. The watering tank he'd invented to take care of the housekeeper's plants wasn't working right, and the woman was in fits over it.

"My herbs'll dry up. See how you'll like your meals, then, with nothing to add a bit of savor to 'em," she said.

Cap removed the copper watering tank from its hooks on the kitchen wall. It was still full, though it'd been a week since he'd filled it. He pulled each thin rubber tube from the soil inside the pots. The tubes extended from the bottom of the tank to carry a

steady trickle of water to the plants on the windowsills. The boy
frowned down at the tank. Why wasn't it working anymore?

Once the tank was emptied, one glance told him the story. The
holes punched into the bottom were plugged with a hardened
crust, likely from the minerals in the water. Grinning at such an
easy fix, Cap began to chip away at the residue. While he worked,
Mrs. Hardy swept inside, dropping parcels onto the sideboard.

"Glad to see you're attending to that," she said. "It's a wonder,
to be sure, but it does me no good if it stops working. Ah, the talk
in town is a fright, Cap! A stolen body, and they don't know who
did it. Did you say your prayers this morning, now?"

Mutely, Cap nodded. From the corner of his eye, he watched as
Mrs. Hardy made the sign of the cross. A soft muttered prayer
reached his ears. The woman was speaking his name.

Warmth spread through the boy's chest. For all her gruff words
and cuffs to the ear, Mrs. Hardy cared about him. "And protect
him from those devilish men who dig up the dead…"

Cap's shoulders slumped.

That means I ought to ask God to protect me from myself, he
thought ruefully. *But I guess it's not people like me who need protect-
ing. It's folks like Delphia. And Jardine.*

He returned to his work, but a knock on the door interrupted
him. At a pointed look from the housekeeper, Cap rose to answer.

"Hullo there," Mr. Garrett said when the boy opened the door.
"Just the man I wanted to see." He dug a crumpled handkerchief
from his coat pocket and blew his nose, honking like an angry
goose. Then he stood back and revealed the reason for his visit.

Behind him was the large pickle crate Cap had seen the other
day at the watchmaker's shop, sitting on top of a child's wagon.
His spirits rose.

"Do you need help?" he asked with a grin, already moving to heft the box from the wagon.

"I surely do," Mr. Garrett replied, and the two brought the crate inside and set it on the kitchen table.

While Mrs. Hardy bustled about and fussed, Cap opened the pickle crate and examined the device nestled inside. It was a wooden box with wires that stuck out from a small hole. One wire was connected to a gray cylinder a few inches long. The other wires had small metal circles attached to their ends. On the side of the box was a hand crank.

"Stimulation for the nerves," Mr. Garrett said. "Some newfangled treatment for folks who can't walk. Least ways, that's what I was told."

Mrs. Hardy huffed. "A treatment for the crippled?" she said. The woman began to vigorously chop carrots on the sideboard, as though she held a powerful grudge against the vegetables. "I vow it'll never work. Doctors don't know how to fix everything, now, do they? I'm certainly kept busy making my tinctures and remedies, even with all the doctors in this town."

Mamma called from upstairs and the housekeeper wiped her hands upon her apron and hurried from the room.

"So, how does it work?" Cap asked.

"A magnet powers it," Mr. Garrett said.

Cap held his breath when the watchmaker opened the lid of the box. Inside, the crank connected with a metal wheel similar to the tiny ones inside watches and clocks. And the wheel was attached to a horseshoe-shaped magnet.

"So, that magnet makes the shock?" Cap asked.

"Yes sirree."

"Can I try?" the boy asked.

For a while, the two took turns trying to generate a current as they cranked the handle. Mr. Garrett explained his troubles with the invention. "I need a stronger current," he said. "Most it does is make a fellow laugh like he's being tickled. That ain't no good. Besides, it ain't easy keeping those metal bits there stuck to a fellow's legs. They keep falling off."

"Why don't you add another magnet?" Cap said, his mind alive with possibilities. "And put those metal bits onto leather straps so they'll stay right next to a person's skin without falling off."

Mr. Garrett's eyes lit up. "That's the ticket! I think you may be on to something," he said. The man clapped Cap on the back and the boy beamed. At that moment, Father walked into the kitchen.

"What's this?" he asked.

"It's Mr. Garrett's new invention," Cap said. He told his father all about it, tripping over his words in a rush to speak. Father said nothing but nodded politely. But after he helped Mr. Garrett carry his invention outside and waved goodbye to the old watchmaker, Father spoke.

"Old Tom's got a quick mind but not much sense," he said.

Cap frowned. "What do you mean?"

"What's that foolish box good for?" Father said as they returned to the house. "The man's got plenty of useful work, repairing clocks. No need to waste time on such nonsense."

Turning his back, Cap headed to the stairs. For a moment, he considered asking his father if digging up the recently dead to sell to an unknown man counted as "useful work," but he bit his tongue.

Father held him back by placing a hand upon his shoulder. "We've got another job, son," he murmured softly, glancing about to make certain no listening ears were nearby. "Tonight. Go to bed at nine and rest up for a few hours. I'll fetch you when it's time to go."

Cap froze. "So soon?" he said. "But you said we'd lay low for a while."

Father pursed his lips. "There's still no watch at the cemetery. And this body won't be missed—no family at all, to speak of." He squeezed his son's shoulder and hurried down the hallway toward the warm kitchen.

One with no family at all? Cap scowled at their ugly, faded red wallpaper. Did Father mean to say they were stealing the body of an orphan? His stomach muttered a gurgling complaint.

It couldn't be *her*. But still, Jessamyn hadn't been in school the past two days.

Cap grimaced and held his stomach. "This body won't be missed" was what they'd told him the *last* time.

SIX

LATER THAT NIGHT, Cap and Father snuck from their silent house and headed to the cemetery. Once there, they led the rattling wagon through the maze of stone and wood markers until they reached the new grave. As Cap had suspected, this grave was near the one they'd dug up the other night.

"Hello there," Lum said as they approached. "Tonight, we'll dig through this here dirt they just dug up this afternoon. Still soft. No need to dig a blasted tunnel, like I told you."

As he hefted his shovel from the wagon, Cap snorted in disgust. Leave it to Lum to take credit for another fellow's idea.

They dug for nearly an hour. Cap started at every sound: wind rustling and clacking in the branches of the nearby trees, a dog's howl from the farms off to the west, and Hilda, the old mare's gentle snorts. But they remained alone. Finally, their shovels scraped against wood.

"I'll open the coffin," Lum said, once they had cleared away enough soil. "Noah, get me that crowbar."

Clambering out of the grave, Cap smiled wryly to himself. Never mind Lum stole his idea, at least he'd never have to crawl into a black tunnel again to pull out a body. He rubbed an aching shoulder and went to stroke Hilda's side while Lum broke open the coffin.

"Got it," Lum called. "Here, Noah, grab that carpet. I'll toss the thing up to you."

Within moments, the soft *thud* told Cap that the body was safely in the wagon bed.

"Don't forget her clothes, Noah," Lum called.

Cap's heart thumped painfully as the realization hit him. *Her* clothes. It was a woman. Or a girl.

Of course, Jessamyn wouldn't be buried in this part of the cemetery, he told himself. He frowned as he stabbed his shovel into the mound of dirt. They'd only worked for a few moments when Lum seized his arm in a painful grip. "What was that?" the man hissed.

Cap froze, his ears straining for the slightest sound. Then he heard it: a horse's hooves, clopping ever nearer at a fast pace. They were discovered again!

"Into the wagon, quick!" Lum shouted. He extinguished the lantern.

Cap turned to run, banging his foot on the blade of the shovel he'd just dropped. Cursing under his breath, he hurled himself in the direction of the wagon. He nearly missed it but caught his ribs painfully on a corner of the box.

The horse galloped ever nearer. "You there, stop!" a man's voice shouted. Then the horse squealed and must have reared, for a solid *thud* echoed through the wintery air, followed by a cry of pain.

Father seized Cap's arm and hoisted the boy into the back of the wagon, right on top of the dead passenger. He clambered over the slight, carpet-bundled form and hunched down next to his father. Lum whipped Hilda, and the aging mare took off.

"Stop!" Their pursuer shouted once more, his voice now shrill. "Stoooop!"

But good old Hilda was fast. Clouds parted to reveal a sliver of moon, which illuminated the cemetery with its small leaning markers. Bare tree branches flashed by as they fled, tipping in the wind as though they waved goodbye with bony fingers.

Frantic shouts quickly died out behind them. Soon, Lum's deep-throated chuckle floated into the night. "Lost him," he said.

"You said there'd be no watch," Father said. "The girl had no family."

"Blamed if I know why anybody'd care for this one," Lum said.

They drove for a few frantic minutes until Hilda's hooves clopped along the cobbles of paved streets. Suddenly, the wagon shuddered to a halt as Lum jerked on the reins. Cap peered out above the rim of the box. They were next to the castle-like building of City Hall. The place bustled with activity.

"At this time of night? Quick, man," Father hissed. "Move on! Someone will see us! Go!"

Uttering a string of oaths, Lum whipped poor Hilda once more, and they moved forward with a jolt. They moved at a fast clip for a few minutes, then made a sharp turn into a narrow passage Cap recognized. His heart sped up. They were heading to the Round House. The abandoned brick farmhouse was haunted. Everyone said so. Though he was old enough to have outgrown the fear of ghosts, Cap instinctively shrank lower in the wagon bed.

"It's all lit up here, too, like Independence Day," Lum muttered in a loud whisper. "What does he want us to do, waltz right in there bold as brass with this thing?"

"What should we do?" Father asked.

"Let's find out what's going on," Lum growled. "You stay here, boy," he told Cap. The two men scuttled like overgrown rats around the house and out of sight.

The boy jerked off his coat and shoved up his sleeves, kneeling beside the rolled carpet. At least he had time to see who this was. There was just enough light from the doorway for Cap to see her features.

He raised the edge of the carpet and pulled it away from the corpse's face, and his heart turned to a lump of ice.

"No," he moaned, falling back on his heels.

Though daubed with mud and leaves, strands of the young girl's thick, raven-wing hair gleamed in the wan light. Her oval face was serene, and she seemed to be asleep. It was indeed Jessamyn.

Darkness flooded Cap. "Not you," he whispered. The girl's still face fractured and dissolved as tears welled up. How could this be? How had the girl come to be buried in the colored section of the cemetery?

Cap wiped his arm across his burning eyes. He wouldn't cry like a child! Then, he gritted his teeth. He wouldn't hand her over, either. Jessamyn deserved a proper burial, and hang the consequences!

Cap hopped into the box of the wagon. Nudging Hilda, he turned the wagon and headed back into the alley. The old Catholic church, now an orphanage but still called St. Joseph's, was only a few blocks away. He'd leave Jessamyn at the back door.

Pulling to a stop in front of the back steps of the old church, he climbed into the wagon box for one more look. She was as serene as before, eerily beautiful in the dim moonlight.

"Why can't you be sleeping? Just sleeping?" Cap whispered. Without thinking, he reached down to touch her cheek. As he did so, the feeling of warmth upon his fingers shocked him, causing the hair on the back of his neck to stand up.

Cap gasped and pulled his hand away, and in that moment, Jessamyn's eyelids fluttered. It was a slight movement, no greater than a flicker.

Am I dreaming this? Cap stared down and waited, but saw nothing.

Hardly daring to breathe, he reached down again and touched the girl's soft cheek, then placed his palm on her forehead. She was still. So very still. A girl carved in stone.

Moments passed. Leaves skittered in the wind as Cap waited with wide eyes. His heart started to sprint. He counted the beats. Ten. Fifteen. Thirty-two. His heart slowed.

Finally, he let his hand fall away. Jessamyn was dead. Cap cursed himself for being a fool—one who saw things he desperately wanted to believe. He sat back on his heels and reached down to cover her face.

Then, she opened her eyes.

Cap screamed.

SEVEN

T HE GIRL'S EYELIDS fluttered and closed again. Before Cap
could take another breath, the heavy back door of the orphanage scraped open.

"Who's there?" a tremulous voice demanded.

Cap pointed to where Jessamyn lay in the wagon. An elderly
woman in a ragged shawl and a nightgown edged closer until she
saw the girl.

"God have mercy," she gasped. "Jessamyn!" Her eyes grew
round as buttons, and then she whirled and hurried to the door,
shrieking: "Help! Sisters, help me!"

A flood of women in nightgowns spilled from the door and
clustered around the wagon. One of the younger ones gently lifted
Jessamyn and carried her inside.

Cap grabbed the reins, ready to hustle out of there, but a hand seized his wrist. He yelped.

"Come with us," a deep voice commanded. Before he could gather his wits, Cap was pulled from the seat of the wagon and hurried inside by a short and very round woman who dragged him along with an iron grip on his arm.

The back door led into a kitchen, where embers still glowed inside a huge fireplace. Swept along quickly, the woman pulled Cap down a corridor and up a creaking wooden staircase. She brought the boy into a small bedroom, where Jessamyn lay upon the bed.

Cap's arm began to tingle. He pulled away, and the hand that had held him finally let go. Without sparing him a glance, the woman issued curt orders to others who had followed them.

"Send for the doctor," she said, and one of the sisters rushed from the room. "And then wake—no," she said, as though to herself, "not now." She glanced at Cap and then away. "Be certain to wake no one else." The women nodded gravely and left.

Inching toward the door, Cap tried to make his escape, but the woman swiftly blocked his exit with her wide body. With a quick, imperious gesture, she indicated the chair in the corner.

The boy backed up and sat. Then the woman smiled at him. She had a broad, lumpy face, pale and round as a full moon, with a dark shadow of a moustache on her upper lip. Despite her ugly features, Cap sensed something about her that calmed his fears, if only a bit.

"What is your name, child?" she asked.

"Captain Cooper," Cap said.

The woman raised her eyebrows and blinked, studying his face for a moment with a strange expression. Then, she turned without a word and held her candle aloft as she moved to the bed and gently felt Jessamyn's forehead.

"And how did you come to be here in the dead of night, with our Jessamyn in the back of your wagon?" the woman asked.

Cap opened his mouth to answer, but before he could say anything, the door opened and Dr. Ivins swept inside.

"I came straightaway," he said, breathing hard as if he'd been running for miles. His shirt was rumpled and his boots were muddy.

"Thank you, Doctor," the woman said. "Bless you."

Dr. Ivins took Jessamyn's wrist to take her pulse, and gently lifted one eyelid. Reaching into his bag, he took out a small vial and gave it to the woman who had remained standing beside him, hovering like a guardian gargoyle. The man's hands shook like autumn leaves in a windstorm. The woman clasped the doctor's hands briefly in her own.

"This is a shock for all of us," she said.

Dr. Ivins nodded and cleared his throat. Then he turned and saw the boy for the first time.

"Cap?" he said. "Why are *you* here?"

"I found her," the boy blurted, trying to imagine a story the two would believe without telling what had actually happened.

"Where?" Dr. Ivins said in a sharp voice.

"On the street," Cap said in a rush of inspiration. "I ... I couldn't sleep and was looking out my window. I saw someone walking about, looking confused." Swiftly, he told them a story of finding the girl and helping her into his wagon, then taking her to the orphanage.

The woman rushed over to Cap and enfolded him in a hug.

"We're so grateful to you, child," she said. Her eyes gleamed with tears. "We thought that we'd lost our sweet Jessamyn. She came down with a fever a few days ago, and Dr. Ivins was away. That dreadful Dr. Rusch came, but he was no help. She grew worse and worse, until she died."

"Died?" Cap repeated, as if he didn't already know.

"We had a service for her, here. We're her family, you see. After, she was taken to the cemetery. I cannot imagine how..." Her voice trailed off, and she looked at the doctor with a crinkled brow, but quickly looked away and dabbed at her eyes with a handkerchief.

Dr. Ivins cleared his throat and reached out to pat the woman's shoulder. "We will speak later. This girl needs to rest. Come, Cap," he said, motioning to the boy. "I'll accompany you outside."

"God be with you both," the woman said as they stood to go.

Cap followed the doctor outside. Loyal Hilda stood placidly in place, snorting and flicking her tail. Dr. Ivins said nothing until Cap had hopped up onto the wagon seat and picked up the reins.

"We're grateful for your help, young man. Now, hurry home. If your mother awoke and found that you were gone, the distress wouldn't be good for her health."

"No, sir."

"Off with you." The doctor slapped Hilda's side, and she trotted away.

The boy hunched his shoulders against the frigid air as he drove. Now, he had a new problem. What in tarnation could he say to Father and Lum?

Tell them what happened, Cap scolded himself. *That's all there is to do.*

But what *had* happened? The sudden warmth, the flutter of the girl's eyes—and then, she was alive again! And what's more, Cap had been the one to bring her back. He was certain.

A strange memory lit up his mind the moment the girl opened her eyes. This wasn't the first time the boy had heard of a person coming back from the land of the dead. Not at all. Because almost thirteen years earlier, someone else had been brought back to life. And that someone was Cap.

He parked the wagon and had just hopped down from the seat when a hand seized him by the arm.

"Where'd you go, boy?" Lum hissed. "Quick, now. I found one of my fellows. He'll meet us at the mouth of the lane and take the stiff. We best hurry—a man escaped from jail so the town's crawling with lawmen."

Cap scowled. What had just happened was too near to the heart to share. He didn't want to even speak Jessamyn's name aloud for ugly old Lum to hear. Besides, they wouldn't understand.

"It's already done," he blurted.

"What?" Father and Lum spoke at the same moment. Lum darted to the side of the wagon and swore when he saw the empty carpet.

"Someone already took the goods," Cap said.

Lum kicked the wagon wheel. "So, where's our payment?" he asked.

Cap froze. "He said that they'd pay us later," he mumbled.

"Those pigs," growled Lum. "I was looking forward to a pint at Mooney's."

"Come," Father said. "We must leave. It's getting nigh on to morning, and the town will be waking soon. Well done, son." He ruffled Cap's hair.

Morning sunrise spilled liquid gold onto the streets as they passed, and a shower of falling leaves rained down on Cap's head.

He barely noticed. Instead, he itched for the day to come. There was someone he needed to speak to. Someone who just might know how Cap came to possess a power that could bring back the dead.

EIGHT

B ACK HOME, CAP collapsed onto his bed but only slept in
brief snatches. The night's events whirled and spun like a
child's toy top inside his head, so it was nearly impossible to rest.
Jessamyn's dark eyes, fluttering open and closing again, haunted
his brief dreams.

When the household finally began to stir, he threw off his
blankets. He dumped water from his chipped pitcher into the ce-
ramic basin on the dresser and quickly scrubbed graveyard dirt
from his face and wavy blond hair. While he washed, the church
bells rang in town.

At least it's Sunday, he thought with a grin. *No Master Rankin
giving me his squinty-eyed stare at school. Besides, I've got to talk to
someone right away.*

Then Cap's smile faded. He was thrilled Jessamyn was alive, but Father and Lum were supposed to have earned a nice payment for the body of someone who wasn't dead anymore. He dried his face and crept to the hall, careful to tiptoe on stockinged feet. He had to figure out *something* about that payment.

Upon the stairs, the smell of freshly baked bread filled his nose. Cap's stomach complained loudly of its empty state. He headed first to the kitchen for a quick bite. After all, he could hardly think when his gullet was empty.

On the blue-checked tablecloth, warm loaves were lined up in a neat row, tan and rounded. The shape of the bread called to mind a row of freshly dug graves, but it smelled heavenly in the kitchen. As he reached for a loaf, he spied a newspaper on the table, its headline screaming in thick, black letters:

Another Empty Grave!
Gang of Ghouls Strikes Again!

Cap snatched up the paper and scanned the article. The newspaper men didn't know who'd been buried in the empty grave. The article mentioned that the medical college in Columbus had answered the telegraph sent after Nellie's grave was robbed. The school firmly denied buying any bodies. And a side article told how the residents in Nellie Jackson's neighborhood were asking the city to place a guard at the cemetery.

If the school in Columbus isn't buying the bodies, well, where are they going? Cap wondered. At that moment, Mrs. Hardy swept into the room with an apronful of potatoes. The boy dropped the paper as though it seared his fingers.

"Ah, you're up, and filthy, by the sight of you! You could grow carrots in your ears and onions on the back of your neck." The woman shook her head. "Sit. I'll get your breakfast."

"Is Father here?" Cap asked Mrs. Hardy as she placed a steaming bowl of oatmeal porridge before him.

"He's gone on business. Said he'd return at noon," she answered, now setting a plate of toasted bread with apricot preserves at his elbow. The housekeeper turned away and began to crush herbs in a tiny bowl, singing softly to herself.

As he wolfed down his meal, Cap's mind whirled. What in tarnation would he say to Father when he came home?

Perhaps I should just tell him the truth about what happened, he thought. But his spirits sank at the thought. *He wouldn't understand. He won't believe me at all, blast him. Father thinks anything like that is balderdash!*

He leapt to his feet, left his dishes in the stone sink, and fled to his room. His thoughts were a tangle.

He'd barely reached the top of the stairs when the front door flew open and Father hurried inside.

"Cap!" Father bellowed, closing the door behind him with a bang. "Come down!"

The boy stopped short and whirled. Father was back already, and Cap had no money to show for last night. No story to cover his hide, either.

"Come, I've something for you," Father said.

Cap's eyes flew open wide. Father was smiling.

The boy began his descent, blinking in surprise. When he reached the bottom step, Father dug into his pocket and fished out a small object that winked with a metallic gleam. He tossed it into the air, and Cap caught it mid-flight.

It was a coin, one far heavier than the pennies he was used to. He gaped at the object in his palm. It was a dollar. A whole dollar? Cap stared wide-eyed at his father while fearing his legs were about to give out.

"You've earned it," Father said, ruffling his son's wavy hair. He grinned and turned away.

"But how—" Cap said, but more words failed him.

"Lum stopped by and dropped off our share," Father said. "He found his partner and got our payment. They paid him for our first job and last night's together." Father's eyes crinkled as he smiled. He tossed on a hat and threw his coat around his shoulders.

"I'm off to pay our grocer's bill. The man's been on my back about it. Mind you wash up, now. You're filthy." The door swung shut behind him.

Cap gaped at the coin in his hand. It was worth a whole day's wages for a man like Father, who worked at the foundry outside of town. Surely, that meant that Father's payment was, well, more money than Cap could imagine.

Silently, he returned to his room. He stretched out on his bed and stared for several minutes at the water stains in the plaster ceiling.

The immediate problem of payment for an undelivered corpse had been solved, but how? And who in Sam Hill had paid them such a princely sum for a body they never got? It was a puzzle.

Cap didn't stay in bed for long. More questions burned like hot coals inside his brain, and now that he could set aside one problem, it was time to focus on another. Sounds outside his door told him Mamma was finally up. She was the one he'd been fairly itching to talk to. He needed to hear the story of the time he had died.

At his knock, Mamma called for him to enter. His parents' bedroom was sparsely furnished, like the rest of the house, but Cap always found this room welcoming. Vivid autumn leaves stood in a vase on the mantle, and a low fire crackled cheerfully in the grate. The walls were painted a pale green that brought a feeling of spring even in the dead of winter.

"Cap," his mother said, smiling from her rocking chair by the window. She placed her open book on her lap and reached out for him. Cap crossed the room and took hold of her hand. It was cold. Her slim fingers felt like those of a small child.

"How are you, Mamma?" Cap asked.

"Oh, much better. The fever's left me. Jardine is a wonder. I'm so pleased Dr. Ivins found her. She knows as much as he does."

"She was in the kitchen again, rummaging about in *my* cupboards," Mrs. Hardy said as she barged into the room, pausing for the slight tug needed to pull her wide skirts through the narrow doorway. She moved past Cap and placed a tray on the little table beside Mamma's chair.

"She came by this morning to return the book she borrowed and I asked her to make tea, Mrs. Hardy," Mamma replied. "You weren't here yet."

"A book," Mrs. Hardy said. She snorted. "You mean to tell me *those folks* read?"

"Why, of course they do," Mamma said, her face growing troubled. "Jardine quite adores poetry."

"Oh, never mind that," Mrs. Hardy said, as she placed a bowl of broth upon the small table and handed Mamma a spoon. "But what good am I, now, if you can't call for me to come early now and then? There's no need for that woman to come to this house at all hours."

"That woman is my friend, Mrs. Hardy," Mamma said in a quiet voice.

"Of course, Mina," Mrs. Hardy said shortly.

Whistling to himself, Cap sat on the bed and tapped his fingers on the coverlet while Mamma ate. It seemed like an eternity before she finished and Mrs. Hardy left.

The moment the door closed behind the housekeeper, Cap spoke. "Mamma?"

"Yes?"

"Tell me again about the day I was born. On the ship."

Mamma's cornflower blue eyes blinked rapidly. She shifted her long, tawny braid back over her shoulder and sat up taller.

"Whatever made you think of that, Cap?" she asked. Her forehead crinkled in a slight frown.

"My birthday is coming, soon." He only felt a slight twinge at the lie.

"Of course," Mamma said with a smile. Cap sat cross-legged on the floor beside his mother's chair and settled in to listen.

"You came early," Mamma said. "Your father and I were all alone on that ship, but Noah found an old Irishwoman to attend to me. And so, you were born. Oh, you were the darling of the other passengers on that ship! How they doted on you. And, of course, we named you after the ship's captain, who was so kind to us. Tiny as you were, you've grown hale and hearty. Why, just look at you now," she said, reaching down to brush a wayward curl out of Cap's eyes.

"But there's more to it, Mamma," Cap said. "I know there is." He knew because he'd heard it once, as a small boy hidden in a cupboard, his face covered with crumbs of stolen cake. Mamma had whispered the real story to Mrs. Hardy. And Cap needed to hear it now.

Mamma placed a trembling hand to her chest. "Why, Cap, what do you mean?"

"You said I died," Cap said. "I heard you." He rose to his knees and took his mother's hand in his. "Please tell me. Just this one time." He waited, holding his mother's gaze with his own.

Mamma took a deep breath. Her eyes were enormous.

"It's true, Cap," she whispered. "You were so small. So frail. You hardly cried out at all, and the old woman told me to hold you while I could. She vowed you wouldn't last the night. And you ... you didn't."

Cap held his breath, waiting to hear what she would say next.

"Noah knocked on doors up and down the ship, seeking a doctor. He didn't find one, but he met two strange men who said they could help."

"How?" Cap stammered.

"I don't know. You were gone, Cap. You weren't breathing. But one of them placed his fingers on your tiny head and began to pray. I don't recall what he said, but you suddenly grew warm in my arms. Heat poured from your little body and flooded into me as well. Then, you took a breath and opened your eyes."

Cap shivered. Jessamyn's pale face flashed before his eyes, and he relived the strange warmth that traveled up his arm when he'd touched her cheek. Years ago, he had returned to life at the touch of a stranger's hand. Then last night, Cap's touch seemed to bring Jessamyn back from the grave.

Beat the Devil! Cap thought. *That stranger must have passed some sort of power on to me.*

"Oh, Cap," Mamma said. "Mind you don't tell your father that I told you about this. He does not like to speak of it." She smiled at her son. "If only..." her voice trailed off.

Cap glanced down. He could have easily finished her words for her. If only the strangers with the healing touch could have been there for the births of her other children—a girl, two boys, all born too soon. The Coopers' house should have been filled with tiny footsteps and laughter.

"Thank you, Mamma," Cap said as he stood. "I need to go somewhere. Is that all right?"

"Of course," Mamma said. "Be back before suppertime."

"Yes, ma'am."

"And Cap?"

Cap paused in the doorway. "Yes, Mamma?"

"You need a bath. Perhaps you should do so before you leave."

His shoulders slumped. "Yes, ma'am."

Before his mother could give him any other chore, Cap took his leave and trudged to the kitchen to find Mrs. Hardy and ask her to heat the water.

It was time to return to the orphanage.

It sure looks like I've got some kind of power, he thought, *but I want to be certain.*

St. Joseph's might not have all the answers, but it was Jessamyn's home. There might be clues of some kind. And Cap was going to get back there today, come hell or high water.

"Or bathwater," he told himself grimly.

NINE

CAP MADE ANOTHER attempt to sweep the hair from his eyes, but the stubborn curls that vexed him refused to budge. At any rate, his hair was clean. He didn't plan to bathe for at least another month.

He crossed the street in front of the orphanage. St. Joseph's was small but still imposing in the daylight. The white-painted stucco building loomed over him, looking like a great bat with two wings that extended out at angles from its body.

As he knocked, Cap tried to remember what he'd planned to say, but before he could blink twice, the door opened.

"Yes?"

With a jolt, Cap recognized the woman who'd taken charge last night when he brought Jessamyn to the back door. Her face crumpled into a grin.

"Cap Cooper, isn't it?" she said.

Clearing his throat, Cap nodded. "I came to see if Jessamyn is all right."

"Come in," the woman said, stepping aside. "She's tired, but I suppose you might have a few minutes to talk."

Once more, Cap found himself climbing the staircase that curved up to the second floor. In daylight, the bare walls of the orphanage were plain but clean, though the faded wallpaper peeled in places. At the top of the stairs, the woman led Cap to the same small room he'd visited before.

"A friend is here to see you," the woman announced, rapping on the door.

Jessamyn sat in a chair by the window. She wore a plain blue dress, and her hair hung in a glossy braid down her back. She turned as they entered. When she saw Cap, the girl crossed the room in three quick steps and threw her arms around his neck.

The boy stopped breathing. Jessamyn smelled of soap and clean linen. Without thinking, Cap raised his arms and hugged her back. An instant later, he dropped his arms to his sides while his face burst into flames.

Jessamyn stepped away, but took hold of Cap's hands. "Thank you," she whispered. "You saved my life."

"Come, sit," the woman said, grinning broadly at the two. Stretched wide in that way, her great slash of a mouth lent her face the appearance of a toad. Cap stifled a giggle.

The woman led him to the chair, and he sat with his spine stiff against the hard backrest. The woman motioned for Jessamyn to sit on her bed, and then she herself sank down beside the girl. The bedsprings groaned alarmingly under her weight.

"I run the orphanage," she said. "You may call me Sister Mariah."

Cap nodded.

"We've all had a bit of a shock, haven't we," Sister Mariah said kindly. Jessamyn looked down suddenly and buried her face in her hands.

"Yes, ma'am," Cap said. He cleared his throat. "Anyway, I came to see if Jessamyn is doing well."

"I am, thanks to you," Jessamyn said, raising a tear-streaked face.

"Yes, Dr. Ivins stopped by earlier and said our dear girl should make a full recovery," Sister Mariah said.

Cap licked his lips, hesitating to ask the big question that trembled there, ready to spill out. Taking a deep breath, he plunged ahead.

"Did Dr. Ivins know how exactly someone could die and come back to life?" he blurted. His heart twisted at the distressed look on Jessamyn's face.

Sister Mariah rose to her feet, while the bed seemed to sigh in relief. She paced slowly across the room as she spoke.

"Dr. Ivins says he cannot explain what happened."

"But she did...*die*," Cap nearly whispered the last word, mindful of the tears that sparkled on Jessamyn's dark lashes and the frightened look in her eyes. "Didn't she?"

Sister Mariah gazed at Cap with a crinkled brow. "Yes," she said. "I witnessed it with my own eyes."

"Golly," Cap whispered.

"My mind is greatly troubled by all this," Sister Mariah continued. "Dr. Ivins saw the papers this morning and is most distressed. Of course, he and I know whose grave was opened but we agreed to keep silent on the subject. We don't need prying newspaper men nosing around here. And I'll ask you, Cap, to keep quiet as well," she added with a stern expression.

"Yes, ma'am."

The woman turned to the window. "Such a mystery," she said softly. Then, she straightened her shoulders and turned around. "Dr. Ivins will have it sorted, somehow. He's gone to question the doctor who was caring for Jessamyn when she grew ill."

"Who was that?" Cap asked.

"Dr. Abraham Rusch," Sister Mariah said. "I don't like the man. He told me I couldn't understand what he was doing, because I'm only a woman. The fool," Sister Mariah huffed, folding her arms across her chest.

A new idea pounced on Cap, and he nearly jumped from his seat in excitement.

What if that old Dr. Rusch is Lum's business partner? He sounds like the sort of fellow who'd be involved in something like that resurrection scheme.

Sister Mariah continued to speak, muttering to herself. "He'd be surprised at what I know, that Dr. Rusch," she said softly. "Oh, yes, he'd be surprised."

Cap barely had time to register the woman's rather strange words, for at that moment she marched to the door. She opened it wide and stood waiting. The boy sighed in resignation.

"Well, I suppose I must go," he said, rising to his feet.

He turned back for one more look at Jessamyn, wishing he could remember what he'd wanted to say to her. He stuffed his hands into his pockets. With Sister Mariah present, there'd have been no chance, anyway.

Jessamyn waved. "I'll see you at school," she said. Her face lit with a sparkling smile.

At the sight, Cap's tongue glued itself to the roof of his mouth as though he'd eaten a large slice of Mrs. Hardy's treacle tart. The best he could muster was a half-wave as the door closed behind him.

"This has been quite a mystery," Sister Mariah said, peering sideways at Cap as they descended the stairs. "I do wonder exactly what happened to our girl."

Shrugging, Cap mumbled a quick "Dunno," while his face grew hot.

They arrived at the front door, and Sister Mariah opened it, letting in a wicked breeze that caused her black skirts to billow about her. Cap stepped over the threshold in silence.

"Well, you'd best run on home, child," Sister Mariah told him. "I'm glad to see that you washed. You were a sight to behold last night—you and Jessamyn both, with leaves in your hair and mud streaked all over your faces."

With that, she gave Cap a gentle nudge and slowly shut the door, keeping her eyes on his until she was hidden from view. The door closed with a loud *click*.

Cap flinched. The woman's words were clear: She suspected that he wasn't telling the entire story.

TEN

As Cap walked, he fingered the heavy coin in his pocket. Lost in thought, he nearly stepped into the street in front of a brewer's wagon. He jumped back as angry shouts beat against his ears, and the stocky draft horses jostled by only inches away.

"Blast!" he cursed out loud. With a hammering heart, he shook his head to clear away the cobwebs. No sense getting himself squashed under horses' hooves just because he wasn't paying attention.

Stomping his feet to keep them warm, Cap had hardly taken two steps when the door to a nearby saloon opened. A wave of warm and pungent air carried shouts of laughter. "Dr. Abe, don't go! Buy us another round!" someone called.

The boy stopped short. *Dr. Abe? That sure sounds like—*

His thoughts were interrupted as a pale man with protruding teeth and a squashed nose burst outside and stumbled down the sidewalk. His face was flushed with drink.

"Dr. Abe must be off to the hospital, fellows," he bellowed. He passed by Cap without even a glance at the boy.

Ignoring the cold that made his hands and feet ache, Cap followed. This drunken doctor had to be Dr. Rusch. He was the man who'd treated Jessamyn and declared her dead.

The doctor never once glanced back. After a few minutes, the man veered left without warning and entered an alley between two crumbling buildings. Puzzled, Cap closed the distance. He peered around the wall where the man had disappeared. About ten feet away, Dr. Abe's dark coattails were vanishing inside a dilapidated brick building. A splintered wooden door creaked shut behind him.

Cap crept forward. Garbage was piled high at his feet, and he had to pick his way carefully to avoid slipping on the slimy remains of rotting vegetables. But before he reached the door, the doctor stepped outside and locked it behind him.

He stopped short as he whirled and spied the boy.

"Who are you?" he asked, gazing down at Cap and blinking as if his eyes couldn't quite focus. He adjusted a pair of wire rim glasses perched on the end of a nose that looked like a miniature pumpkin. Several rings set with colorful stones sparkled on the man's fingers.

"Dr. Rusch?" Cap asked, ignoring the man's own question.

The man stared without a word.

"I'm sorry to trouble you, but I wanted to ask about—"

"Off with you! I'm busy!" Dr. Rusch roared. He flung his arm forward and caught Cap across the chest. The boy lost his balance and plopped onto the trash-strewn ground.

Dr. Rusch reached the street and continued his unsteady march toward the hospital. Simmering like a kettle about to boil, Cap rose to his feet and followed again, picking bits of egg shell from his trousers.

I don't care beans if he doesn't want to talk to me, he thought, gritting his teeth. *I'm not through with him, no sir!*

The streets were busy with Sunday churchgoers. Keeping the doctor in sight, Cap dodged in and out of small knots of people dressed in their best. Soon, they arrived at the hospital. He watched as the doctor hurried inside and counted to ten before following.

Once through the doors himself, Cap glanced about, but the man had somehow whisked himself away. A hallway stretched out ahead, and a steady stream of people moved about the place.

"Well, hello, Cap. We meet again, don't we?" someone said.

Cap whirled and met the friendly gaze of Dr. Ivins. His tall form was dressed as usual in clothing that was clean but threadbare. The man's tired face wore a quizzical expression.

"Oh, hello, Dr. Ivins," Cap said. Then, he added with a sudden burst of inspiration: "I'm looking for Dr. Rusch. I have a message for him."

The doctor's eyes widened, and he blinked. Then, he motioned for Cap to follow. The boy hurried after him down the narrow hall. Cap's mind whirled. He had to come up with a message, and fast! He wrinkled his nose as they picked their way around a small pile of bloody bandages on the floor.

Dr. Ivins opened a door and led Cap to the grounds outside. He squinted in the bright fall sunshine as he hurried after the tall man. "Where's Dr. Rusch?" Cap asked.

"I suppose you're wondering why I took you away from the hospital. I'm worried about the illness that has struck our town. We have seven new cases this morning," the doctor said, rubbing a hand over his chin.

"What illness?" Cap asked.

The crease between the doctor's eyebrows deepened. "It calls to mind the terrible yellow fever epidemic of last century. It's a dreadful thing, Cap," he said, gazing down at the boy. "And why I moved you out of the hospital so quickly. You would not want to catch this illness, nor would you wish to bring it home to your mother."

"No, sir." Cap breathed. He gulped and jammed his hands into his pockets to keep them from trembling. Then, a new idea struck him.

"Did Jessamyn have that illness?"

The doctor blinked. "I don't know," he finally said, "as I did not treat her. Perhaps." The man rubbed his tired eyes. "It is dreadful, Cap. Keep away from the hospital and from anyone who grows ill. Now, then," he added, straightening his crumpled cravat and smoothing his hair, "Whatever message you have for Dr. Rusch, you may tell me," he said in a lighter voice.

Cap's stomach flipped over like a flapjack on a hot skillet, since he'd had no time to create any story. He took a deep breath. "I, uh, sir, you see ..." Words failed him, and he dropped his gaze to his scuffed boots, his heart sinking.

But then a miracle happened. Dr. Ivins said, "Perhaps you bring Dr. Rusch news of his mother? She promised to send word when she arrived in town."

Wordlessly, Cap nodded.

"Ah, good. I'll tell him."

Cap's heart stuttered in his chest. *Oh, St. Mary*, he thought. *What'll old Rusch think when he finds out his mother isn't here?* Cap resisted the urge to smack himself on the forehead.

"Well, I must return to my work," Dr. Ivins said, putting a hand on the hospital door. "Goodbye." With that, the man disappeared inside the hospital.

Cap headed home in the cold, purple-tinged twilight. He'd learned nothing from following Dr. Rusch, though he did wonder about that strange brick building. What was in there?

He sobered and slowed his steps as he neared his neighborhood. The tired face of Dr. Ivins came to mind. *Seven* new cases of that strange new illness. Cap wrapped his arms tightly about his body, while a jumble of fears made his head ache. If folks in Circleville kept falling ill from that deadly sickness, the town's newest resurrectionists might end up with more work than they'd ever imagined.

ELEVEN

T HE KITCHEN WAS empty. Mrs. Hardy had rushed off to care
for a sick cousin and had left a simple meal of cold meat and
boiled potatoes. Cap peeked into Mamma's room but she was
sleeping, so he closed the door softly. He and Father sat down to
eat together. Father wolfed his food and moved into the front
parlor to smoke his vile-smelling pipe that made the house reek.

Left to himself, Cap munched on a heel of bread and paced the
kitchen, trying to untangle his thoughts. New bunches of herbs
hung from the ceiling near the iron stove, drying out for storage.
Cap fingered a bundle of spiky leaves, and the pungent scent of
rosemary filled the air.

A pang of sadness filled him. Mrs. Hardy's herbs helped plenty
when one of the family had a cold or an upset stomach. The thing

was, they didn't help Mamma at all when she gave birth too early to the tiny babies who died within minutes of entering the world.

Please, God, let this time be different, he prayed silently.

A soft rap at the front door made him jump. Father's quick footsteps sounded in the hall, and low voices rumbled like thunder heard over distant hills. Then, the front door closed and Father poked his head into the kitchen.

"We've another job to do this evening," he whispered. "We'll leave now, as your mamma is asleep. Looks like a storm's rolling in. Wear your wool coat."

Caught off guard, Cap surprised himself by nearly laughing aloud. He clapped a hand over his mouth, quickly turned the laugh into a cough, and pounded on his chest for good measure.

"Yes, sir," he managed to croak out. Without raising his head to look at his father, he squeezed past him and hurried upstairs, taking care to miss the step that always squealed like a mouse caught in a trap.

We'll just see what happens, Cap thought, yanking his coat from its nail inside his wardrobe and pulling on his scarf. *Yes sirree, we will. If I have power to raise the dead, I should be able to do it again, tonight.*

Nearly afire with nervous energy, Cap hurried downstairs and out into the winter night. Father was right about the weather. An icy rainstorm doused them but good. Freezing needles of water dripped down the back of Cap's neck as he dug, spurring him to work faster. Sweating and swearing, the two older men dug furiously as well. Finally, they reached the coffin and broke it open.

Moving this body from its eternal rest took some effort, thanks to the man's weight. The resurrectionists were forced to tie a rope about him and pull together to remove him from the deep hole.

Finally, the stocky corpse emerged from the earth and slid to a stop in the thick mud beside the wagon.

"Now I know how my mother felt when she birthed me into the world," Lum said, wheezing. "Said I right near killed her 'cause I took a day and a half to come out. She could hardly stand the sight of me for a week."

"No surprise that, with your fat head," Father muttered, softly so only Cap could hear. The boy pressed his lips together to keep from grinning as the men hurriedly stripped the corpse's mud-filled clothing from his body.

Cap squinted at the body in the dim lantern light. The corpse's downy hair was white, and his pockmarked brown face bore the deep lines of a man who'd seen many years and many troubles.

"What are you doing, lazybones?" Lum said. "Help us lift this man into the wagon. He weighs as much as an ox."

Squeezing his eyes shut, Cap tugged the gloves from his hands and tossed them to the ground.

This is it, he thought. He reached down and grabbed the man's ankles, while Noah and Lum lifted the man by his arms. Cap waited for the warm sensation he'd felt when he'd touched Jessamyn's face. But with the man's ankles coated in cold mud, he had no idea whether anything was happening.

"One, two—" Father counted aloud.

The man screamed.

They dropped him, and the grown men screamed back.

"What in the Sam Hill?" Lum shouted. He fell to his backside and scrabbled away in the mud. Father seized the lantern and opened the shutters wide as he held the light aloft to illuminate the form on the ground.

The dirt-daubed man's eyes were round as dinner plates. He stared about in a panic. Then he raised shaking hands to his face and felt along his naked, muddy body.

"Where am I?" he croaked. "Where are my clothes? Where's Mary? Find Mary, I want Mary!"

Cap stared with his hands clapped over his mouth. Delighted shock and elation glowed inside. He could have hollered for joy, but he figured he'd best pretend to be as addled as the others.

For a few moments, no one moved. The man blinked at the bright light, shivering and jabbering. Finally, Cap found his shovel and dug about in the grave to fish out the man's clothing. Father helped the man don his filthy and sodden trousers and shirt. Lum was nowhere to be found as Father and Cap helped the man into the back of the wagon.

"Where do you live?" Father asked.

The man told them. It was not far from Cap's own quiet neighborhood. The boy closed his eyes as they jostled along in the wagon, while his mind filled with wonder. Jessamyn had come to life at his touch, and now, so had this man.

If I can do this, I can save Mamma's baby, he thought, his heart chugging like a steam engine at full speed. *I can save everyone!*

"Here we are," Father announced, bringing the wagon to a halt. Cap snapped out of his reverie. He and Father helped the man to his front door. It was far past midnight. The tiny box of a house was dark, and all was quiet except for the continued patter of the freezing rain that fell in their eyes.

They knocked repeatedly. Several long moments passed, but shuffling footsteps finally approached the door.

"Blast! The shock must have addled my brain. What was I thinking?" Father said, turning to Cap with wide eyes. "We never should've—"

The door swung open to reveal an elderly woman with a frizzled, gray-streaked braid that hung over one shoulder.

"Jedediah!" she screamed. "Dear God Almighty!"

She fainted and fell in a heap at their feet.

TWELVE

CIRCLEVILLE CHRONICLER,
NOVEMBER 15, 1875

Ghouls Do a Good Deed; Stiff Turns Out to Be Alive

Our town's mysterious gang of body snatchers are at it again, but this time the laugh was on the thieves. Jedediah Greeves, lately passed on to a better place, has returned from beyond. It seems he was removed last night from his so-called final resting place. The devilish snatchers were certainly startled to find their quarry alive!

O N MONDAY, CAP headed to school in a daze, his mind fogged with weariness. He yawned as he hung his coat and scarf in the cloakroom, wondering if he'd ever get enough sleep again. The only bright point was when Jessamyn turned around to smile at him from her desk.

Cap didn't remember any of his morning lessons. Twice he was called upon to answer Master Rankin's questions, and twice he had to admit he hadn't been listening. He was made to solve several difficult arithmetic problems at the board for his lack of attention.

Finally, the dinner break came, and Cap bolted from his seat. After his dismal display all morning, he wasn't about to face Jessamyn or anyone else. However, when he reached the door, the girl called his name.

"Cap, wait!"

He froze, one foot still a few inches off the floor, while the room filled with whispers.

"Will you walk with me?" Jessamyn asked.

"Yes," Cap said in a loud voice. The whispers increased and someone giggled.

"Shouldn't you save your courting for after school?" Eli called out.

Cap didn't turn around, but simply followed Jessamyn as she headed to the cloakroom, while laughter floated in after them.

"Pay them no mind," he said as they put on their coats.

"I don't," Jessamyn said in a quiet voice as they left the school. "At least, I try not to. Sister Mariah always says that we should only worry what God thinks of us, not what anyone else thinks. I try not to pay those boys any mind at all."

"Well, I mind," Cap said, balling his hands into fists and shoving them into his pockets. "I'd like to smash my fist right into Eli's smeller."

Jessamyn laughed, and Cap put his mind to think of something else clever to say. Unfortunately, he could not imagine a single thing. He kicked a pebble in disgust.

They walked along Walnut Street. Cap pushed aside the thought that he was supposed to head home for his noontime meal. He wasn't about to go there *now*.

"I wanted to thank you again, Cap," Jessamyn said. She brushed a stray hair from her eyes. The boy squelched the urge to reach out and touch the long, wavy strand. "I know you go home at dinnertime, so I won't keep you, but I need your help. You see, I'm missing something very dear to me, and Sister Mariah said you might be able to help me find it."

"What is it?" Cap asked. They stood for a moment in the warmth that emanated from the open doorway of a druggist's shop.

"When I was buried, I wore a ruby ring on my finger. It belonged to my mother, and it's all I own in the world."

"A ring?" Cap said. He hadn't remembered a ring, but they wouldn't have taken it even if they *had* seen it. Lum was strict in that regard. They were not thieves.

"It was a ruby ring from my father," Jessamyn said. "I always wore it on my right hand. When I felt well enough to think clearly, I realized it was gone."

"You think *I* took it?" Cap asked. He stopped in his tracks and turned to face the girl. "I swear to you, Jessamyn, I didn't!"

"Oh, no, Cap, I don't think that at all," Jessamyn answered. "Sister Mariah told me to ask you for help since you're my friend, and you know what happened to me."

"Oh," the boy said. A smile tugged at the corners of his mouth. *Friend.* He sure liked the sound of that. "Of course, I'll try to help," he said. "Where should we start?"

"Some of the Sisters think the sexton must have taken it. They all swear the ring was on my finger when they closed my casket." Jessamyn shivered and continued down the street. Cap followed, clenching his fists as a new suspicion tickled the back of his mind.

If the sexton didn't take it, what if old Lum did? He preaches to Father and me about not stealing from the dead, but I sure wouldn't put it past the old man to snatch a ring like that. He could've done it on the sly.

Taking a deep breath, Cap spoke. "We might talk to the sexton," he said, stepping around a small child pulling a wooden duck on a string. "But I bet you a whole dollar he'll say he didn't take it."

"I thought of that," Jessamyn said. "That's why I talked to Sister Mariah about it. She said you're so clever, you'll surely help me think of a way to discover what happened. Do you think you might?" she asked.

Cap gazed into the girl's troubled eyes. "I'll sure try to think of something," he said.

"Thank you," Jessamyn said. She squeezed his hand for a moment. "Why don't we both think of ideas and talk tomorrow at school? Maybe we could even speak to Sister Mariah together."

Cap couldn't keep from smiling broadly as he nodded.

He walked her back to the school, where she turned away with a wave and another quick flash of a grin.

Cap sprinted home for his dinner. Mrs. Hardy's scolding fell on deaf ears. As he ate, he kept reliving the feel of the girl's hand in his. Gulping his milk and wiping his mouth on the back of his hand, he swore on all the Holy Family he'd find a way to help her.

Then, with his mouth full of cold roast beef sandwich, Cap nearly choked. Sister Mariah told Jessamyn to ask Cap for help because he knew what had happened to her.

His shoulders tensed and his breath caught in his throat. Cap recalled the strange way the woman had closed the door, locking her eyes on his as she waited for his reaction to her words.

And what had she said? *"You were a sight to behold last night— you and Jessamyn both, with leaves in your hair and mud streaked all over your faces."*

Sister Mariah most certainly suspected him of something. But what did she suspect? Cap swallowed, and the bread and meat scraped down his throat.

Sister Mariah said she wondered how in the world Jessamyn got out of her coffin, he thought. *She knows. Somehow, she knows I dug Jessamyn from her grave.*

THIRTEEN

Aᴼᴛᴇʀ sᴄʜᴏᴏʟ, Cᴀᴘ hurried to the cemetery, harboring a half-formed idea to spy on the sexton for a while. Bent low against the freezing wind, he was warmed by a tiny spark of hope—if he found that missing ring all on his own, he wouldn't have any reason to visit Sister Mariah again.

Besides that, maybe Jessamyn would squeeze his hand again. Or hug him.

He passed the tall gates of the entrance and hurried to the ramshackle building at the far end of the field where the sexton lived. Despite the cold, lots of folks were out, bundled up and chatting together. In their dark winter coats, they looked like a flock of oversized crows fluttering among the headstones.

Probably on the lookout for more empty graves, Cap thought with a sinking feeling in his gut.

When he got to the sexton's house, no one answered his knock, so he stood on tiptoe and peered into the single window. Nothing was visible through the hazy glass.

"Hullo there, son."

Cap whirled at the sound of Lum's voice.

"Strange goings on, eh?" the man said. He sauntered over and leaned against the rough boards. "Plenty of talk in town about that geezer who come back to life. I reckon that's why all them folks is out there," he added, nodding his head toward the people in the distance.

Cap nodded, keeping his gaze lowered to his boots. The strange goings on were *his* doing, and he could imagine what Lum would say if he knew.

"Never saw nothin' like it before, but I talked to a fellow I know. Says it happens sometimes. Folks buried alive. Maybe the old man was just sort of sleeping, like. Hardly breathing, you know?" Lum chuckled and scratched at the sparse blond hair standing at attention on the top of his head. "So, his wife thought he'd already flown off to meet St. Peter, and she done called someone to take him away. I tell you, I needed a pint or two at Mooney's after that ruckus."

Doubt jabbed like a needle into Cap's chest as the idea seared into his brain. Was *that* what had happened? Air leaked from his lungs, and his entire body wanted to slump.

"But I swear the old man was dead," Cap said. "He didn't move or breathe, and he sure didn't smell too good."

Lum guffawed. "Don't I know it," he said. "But I guess we was all wrong. Anyhow, your pa was daft to take the codger back to his house." Lum turned his head to spit. "Noah shoulda had the sense to leave that old fool be and get his own self away."

Cap clenched his hands into fists.

"At least Father and I didn't run off like scared rabbits," he said.

The next thing Cap knew, his feet dangled a foot above the ground and the back of his head exploded in pain. Lum had grabbed him by his coat and lifted him high, then slammed him into the wall of the small shack.

"I didn't run off scared, boy!" the man hissed, his face inches from Cap's. "I ain't afeared of nothing! You mind your words, or I'll pack you in whiskey and send you off to a place no one'll ever find you. And if they did, they wouldn't know you anyway. You'd be nothing but a jumble of bones!" Before Cap could blink, Lum released him, and he collapsed to the ground.

While the boy gasped for breath, Lum reached into his greasy overcoat. He pulled out a small bundle crusted with dirt and tossed it at the boy's feet. Then he turned his back.

"You'd best learn to not leave your things behind. You never know if someone might recognize them pretty red gloves your sweet mamma made for you."

Lum whistled as he stalked off and Cap glared after him, rubbing the back of his head. Then, he heaved a sigh and hauled himself to his feet.

The wind whistled lonely notes that swirled around the small building, making Cap shiver. His visit to the cemetery hadn't given him any clues about what happened to Jessamyn's ring. All it got him was a run-in with Lum, which left him with an aching head and a mind full of new doubts. Grimacing, he gave the leaning shack a kick before he left.

Saints alive, he thought, groaning as he discovered a new ache in one shoulder. *Do I have power to raise the dead, or don't I?*

When Cap reached his street, a quick glance through the parlor window made him duck down low so the fence would hide him from view. The room was full of ladies sipping from teacups. Mamma was beaming from her chair, holding an open book in her hand.

Cap groaned out loud. Another of Mamma's literary meetings. Last time she'd held a meeting, she'd made him come in and read from a book of Mr. Longfellow's poetry in front of all those ladies. No amount of Mrs. Hardy's fresh ginger snaps could ever make up for that.

Hunched over like an old man with a bent back, Cap snuck past his house. Then, he ran. The blocks leading to Main Street flew by. The boy's pounding feet kept time with his pounding heart. He grew warm and loosened his scarf, but still he ran. Finally, he was too winded to continue. He stopped, gasping for breath, and put hands on his knees.

"Where's the fire?" a girl asked him.

Still wheezing, Cap looked up into a familiar face.

"Oh, hi, Delphia," he said.

"We meet again," the girl said with a laugh. "If you were going to the library, it's closed. Miss Bark isn't feeling well."

Panting for breath, Cap glanced behind the girl to the tall brick building that housed the town's library. The book-filled room was a great source of satisfaction to Mamma, who visited it often when she was well.

"Oh, I didn't come for..." he said, but then stopped while an idea flashed into his head. Was it possible there were books about folks who came back to life after they'd up and died? Besides the Bible, of course. Just his luck the place was closed, right now.

"Well, I *was* going to look for a book," he told Delphia. Even if the librarian wasn't there, he'd bet Delphia had already read every dusty old volume inside that library and then some.

"About what?" Delphia said. The two fell in step together.

"About doctors," he said, thinking fast. "And how they fix people."

Delphia beamed at him as they crossed the street. "Why, Cap, does that mean you want to be a doctor, too?"

"No, it's just," Cap said, thinking fast, "I was thinking about that old man they found alive. How's it possible that a fellow dies but then comes back to life?"

The young woman stopped short and her brow furrowed. "Why, I surely don't know." She glanced down at the thick books in her arms and her lips twisted into a sad smile. "What happened to Mr. Greeves was a wonder. My, I do wish I'd seen the faces of those awful men who dug him up."

Cap forced himself to chuckle, while heat crept into his cheeks.

Delphia looked at him for a moment. "Here," she finally said, pulling a piece of paper from inside one of the books and handing it to Cap. "You hear about that other empty grave they found the other night?"

Jessamyn's grave, Cap thought with a start. *Sure, I heard all about it.* Certain his head was about to burst into flames, he nodded and took the paper. Unfolding it, he read a handwritten letter to the mayor, asking for a guard to be placed at night in the colored section of the cemetery. Names were scrawled at the bottom.

But Jessamyn wasn't one of Delphia's neighbors, he thought, chewing his bottom lip. *Would that make Delphia feel better to know the resurrectionists weren't just digging up her folks?*

Then Cap's whole body burned with guilt.

That doesn't change the fact that we're digging her friends up in the first place, he told himself miserably.

"You'll sign, won't you?" Delphia asked him, pulling a bit of pencil from her pocket.

"Yes," Cap said quickly, taking the pencil. He was half convinced that lightning would strike him down as he wrote, so the girl would be left standing in front of a smoking hole in the ground, wondering where Cap had gone to. But apparently, at that moment, God was too busy to punish him for being a wicked liar as well as a resurrectionist.

Gulping down his guilt, Cap rapidly scrawled his name, and Delphia took the paper back with a warm smile and thanked him.

"I'm only twelve years old," he told her. "My name won't count."

"I don't think anyone will know," Delphia said, her smile growing. "I want as many names as I can get. There's got to be something folks can do to protect their families."

Silently, the two began to walk again. "You know," Delphia said after a moment, "thinking about your question, Cap, only yesterday I started to read *The History of Medicine*. There just might be something in there about how the dead could be revived."

Their steps had led them to the tree-lined drive in front of St. Joseph's. Delphia smiled at Cap and quickened her pace. "I need to get home, but I'll sure tell you if I find out anything," she said as she walked away.

"Thanks," he called to her.

Turning toward home, Cap glanced over at the bat-like building where Jessamyn lived. At that moment, a man ambled around the side of the stucco building.

With a thudding heart, the boy ducked behind the thick trunk of an oak and peered out at the one person he least wanted to see. Fingering the rising lump on the back of his head, Cap glared.

What in tarnation is old Lum doing here? he wondered.

FOURTEEN

L EAPING OVER THE low fence, Cap went straight to his shop
so Mamma wouldn't know he was home. He made it inside
without being discovered and sat at his worktable, itching to get
busy. Whenever he needed to think, he tried to make something.
He would fiddle with bits of wood, some scrap metal, or the tiny
cogs or gears Mr. Garrett gave him.

The air was cold in the tiny room, but the boy hardly noticed.
He fiddled with the wire he'd wrapped around a curved piece of
metal. As far as he could tell, the object wouldn't be good for anything, but he kept trying to come up with an idea. This was how
he'd invented the copper watering tank for plants, and his warming box for chicks. He started with a vague idea, and then played

with various objects. And once in a while he came up with some-thing that worked.

While Cap wound and unwound the wire, Delphia's words kept playing in his head. *There's got to be something folks can do to protect their families.*

"Like what?" Cap whispered to himself. There didn't seem to be anything in the whole world that would stop ugly old Lum.

He worked with the object for a while, not caring how much time passed. While he continued to fiddle with the wire, some-thing came to him—a story Mr. Garrett had told him, about bury-ing torpedoes during the Civil War.

Why, he thought, *that wire, wrapped the way it was around the metal, could function as a—*

A sharp rap at the door startled him. Cap rose and stretched stiff muscles. "Yes?"

Jardine poked her head inside the tiny room. "Your mamma has called you twice for your supper, Cap."

"Oh," Cap said, blinking. "Where's Mrs. Hardy? And Father?"

Jardine smiled. "Mrs. Hardy is tending to a neighbor, and I don't rightly know where your father is. I stopped in for the lit-erary meeting. Lands, but I do enjoy hearing Mina read. Folks from England sure make the words sound fancy."

Cap stifled a laugh. Mamma's words might sound fancy, but Father, well, Mamma was forever scolding her husband for his rough language.

Jardine's eyes twinkled. "Mina wanted you to recite, too, but you went and made yourself scarce."

Ducking his head, Cap made a show of tidying his tools while he cleared his throat.

"Guess it's too bad I wasn't here," he mumbled.

Jardine chuckled. "Well, there's a plate warming for you on the stove," she told him. "Mina asked me to fetch you since you didn't hear her calling. She's plumb wore out from her meeting, so she's in her room." She paused, holding the door open for Cap.

Cap found himself gently but firmly guided to fetch his dinner. Then, he was herded directly to Mamma's room.

"Cap," Mamma said when she saw him. Her quick smile faded. "Why, what's wrong? You seem so tired."

The boy kissed his mother and then sat at the foot of her bed.

"I'm all right, Mamma," he answered, taking a bite of his bread. But the woman sat up and looked him in the eye. Cap ducked his head.

Finally, his mother sighed. "If you say so, Cap," she said, settling back onto her pillows.

Jardine handed Mamma a steaming cup. "Try this," she said. "It's the raspberry tea I told you about. It should help the baby."

Mamma sipped her tea and smiled. "Mm, that's good. Oh, thank you, Jardine." She took another sip as Jardine sat in a chair beside the bed and Cap started on his meal.

"Are you taking raspberry tea as well?" Mamma asked Jardine.

"Oh, yes," the woman answered. She smiled and rubbed her belly, which Cap noticed for the first time was as round as Mamma's.

Mamma and Jardine chatted softly, but soon, Mamma's attention turned back to her son, as she described Cap's new warming box with a gleam of pride in her blue eyes.

"My goodness, you are a smart boy," Jardine said with a smile.

"He is," Mamma said, fairly glowing, "but he does tend to woolgather at school. By the way, Cap, are you keeping up with your schoolwork these days?"

"Yes, Mamma," he said with a tiny sigh.

"And have you made any friends?"

"Yes," he said, glancing away when Mamma tilted her head and pursed her lips. Jessamyn's face came to mind, and his cheeks grew warm. He *had* made a friend, but he wasn't going to tell Mamma about *her*.

He pushed a bit of meat around on his plate. "When is Father coming home?" he asked, to get Mamma talking about something else.

"He said he'd be late again today," Mamma answered. "Oh, and he told me that Columbus Jones had some work for the two of you to do."

From the corner of his eye, Cap saw a quick movement. Jardine had started to rise from her chair, but then stopped. Her dark eyes glittered in the flickering candlelight, and they held Cap's gaze. The boy could have sworn she was trying to tell him something.

Finally, Jardine looked away. "Well, I'd best be going," she said as she rose carefully from her chair. "I surely enjoyed the literary meeting today. Why don't you get some sleep, Mina? Dr. Ivins will be by in the morning."

At that moment, Father poked his head inside. He nodded to the women and looked pointedly at his son.

"Good night, Mamma," Cap said, rising to his feet. "Good night," he said to Jardine, and followed his father out the door.

"We have another job," Father whispered to Cap once they were in the warm kitchen. "Finish eating and get your coat. I'll meet you outside."

"Wait—" But Father's footsteps faded down the hall and the front door swung open and closed.

Cap set his plate in the sink. The cold remains of his dinner were no longer appetizing.

With a frown, he inspected his hands. Here was the real mystery: Did he have power to raise the dead, or not? Was what had happened to Jessamyn and Mr. Greeves only a coincidence? Or was it something more?

Guess I'm about to find out, he told himself grimly.

FIFTEEN

"THIS ISN'T THE way to the cemetery," Cap said, as the wagon jostled down the dark street. The freezing air stung the boy's face, and he tugged the collar of his coat higher.

"We need scrap iron from the foundry," Father replied.

"Why?"

"You'll see."

At the foundry, the two loaded the wagon with bits of metal. Then, they scavenged heavy rocks from a nearby field.

"What's all this for?" Cap asked. His back hurt and his hands ached from the cold, while at the same time he was sweating beneath the layers of his thick winter clothing.

"This job is different," Father explained, hopping up into the driver's seat and taking the reins. "You'll see."

The two drove a few miles outside of town. Eventually, they approached a grand yellow house covered with gables and towers, surrounded by tall poplars. Father made certain to keep his distance from the crowd of carriages and wagons that lined the drive at the front of the home. They circled around the building and parked in the back near a small wooden door.

"Now, we wait," Father whispered. Soon, an undertaker's carriage pulled up beside them. A pudgy man climbed down from the driver's seat. He nodded at Father and ignored Cap.

"Who's that?" the boy whispered.

"The sexton."

Cap sat up straighter. "Oh," he said, squinting in the man's direction. Were there any rings on his fingers? Ruby rings, to be exact?

The man drew closer. His face was pitted with pockmarks and his pale skin had a greasy look, even in the moonlight. Father held out his hand to shake, and the man removed his gloves. His fingers were bare of rings.

The boy slumped down in the wagon seat, blowing out his breath in a white cloud while the sexton and Father talked. Most men weren't cotton-headed enough to wear stolen jewelry, but Cap had hoped that, by some miracle, the sexton was just that dumb. Anyway, something else rankled worse. It sure didn't look to Cap like he'd get the chance to try reviving a body tonight.

Then, something the sexton said caught his attention, and he swore his ears stood up tall just like a pup's.

"The arrangement was made weeks ago," the sexton was saying.

Cap stretched his mouth wide in a fake yawn while he leaned closer to catch the men's whispers.

"Lum will take the body once the mourners leave, and that's where you two come in. You must help me fill the coffin with stones so nothing will seem amiss at the cemetery."

And, so they did. After the sounds of murmured voices and rustling carriages died away, letting them know the mourners had left the wake, they got to work. Cap and Father helped the sexton fill the empty coffin so it would feel as heavy as before. Lum never once graced them with his presence. The jangling jolt of a wagon driving away, as well as the tune the sexton whistled loudly in the night air, let them know he was already off to deliver his goods.

And Cap was back in bed within an hour, though he didn't fall asleep for a long while as new questions rolled around inside his skull.

Once more, the resurrectionists had "resurrected" another body that didn't come from Delphia's neighborhood.

I guess everybody in town ought to be afraid of us, Cap thought. He frowned. The thought wasn't pleasant. He'd never been the kind to taunt or bully other boys, and he sure didn't relish the thought of making *anybody* scared of him.

Unable to sleep, he leaned on one elbow and fingered a loose thread on his coverlet. Everything was such a puzzle. What sort of person would make an "arrangement" to allow some shady fellow to cart his body away, knowing doctors were itching to carve him up?

"And just what were *you* doing at the orphanage, Lum?" Cap whispered to himself. Plopping onto his back, he pondered a while until a plan came to mind. It would be tricky, and he'd have to make certain his friend was mighty careful, but Jessamyn just might be able to help him solve at least one riddle.

. . .

T HE NEXT MORNING, Cap gulped his cornmeal mush with molasses and hurried to school. He wanted time to speak to Jessamyn before class. He tried to ignore the prick of guilt that poked at his heart. He was supposed to be helping *her*, but here he was, conniving to get her to help *him*.

But Lum just might have taken the ring. He reminded himself of the fact as he hurried along his street, his breath coming out in white puffs. Once at school, Cap waited in the cloakroom until Jessamyn arrived, greeting him with a broad smile.

"I saw the sexton," he whispered as the girl hung up her faded winter coat and placed her dinner pail on the shelf. "Last night."

"You did?" Jessamyn breathed. "Did you talk to him?"

"No," Cap said, shuffling his feet. "But I saw his hands. He wasn't wearing any rings."

The girl's smile faded for a moment, but then she brightened immediately. "He'd never wear my ring," she said. "He wouldn't want anyone to know he'd taken it."

"I agree," Cap said. "But right now, I sure can't think of what else to do, except..." He paused for a moment and ran a hand through his hair.

"What?" Jessamyn asked.

Cap bit his lip. "I'm not real certain, but there's someone else I know who might have taken it."

"Who?" Jessamyn said, her eyes round.

"He's a fellow who works with my father," Cap said. He gathered his slate and books and moved into the classroom, as more students were crowding into the cloakroom, smirking at him and the girl. "We heard he's involved in some kind of business," he lowered his voice and leaned closer, "selling things he stole."

Jessamyn's jaw dropped.

"How do you plan to find out if he took my ring?" she asked him, settling her things inside her desk.

"I was thinking *you* could do it," Cap answered. He held up a hand as Jessamyn's brow crinkled in confusion. "Hear me out. I saw him over at St. Joseph's." Swiftly, he described Lum, and Jessamyn's eyes widened in recognition.

"You mean Mr. Jones?" she said. "He does some work for the Sisters now and then, patching the roof and such. Sister Mariah will want to know he isn't honest. I should tell her—"

"No," Cap blurted. "I mean, if we want to catch him, it needs to be done on the sly. If you say anything to Sister Mariah, she might just up and dismiss him. Then, we'll never know if he took your ring or not."

The girl chewed on a fingernail, deep in thought. "You're right," she said after a moment. "Wait—I know!" she added, with a shy smile curving her lips. "I'll keep a close eye on him. The cook feeds him whenever he comes, and sometimes Sister Mariah sits and talks with him. I think she's trying to save his soul. She reads Bible verses. Maybe if I eavesdrop, I'll learn something."

"You just might," Cap said, "But listen, Jessamyn—he's a real rough sort of fellow. You best be careful around him. Swear to it you'll only listen, and keep your distance."

Jessamyn nodded solemnly, but her eyes gleamed with excitement. "I promise."

"So, you stick to Lum, I mean Mr. Jones, and I'll stick to the sexton," Cap whispered, taking out his history book as Master

Rankin walked to the blackboard, ready to start the school day. "Between the two of us, maybe we'll find your ring."

And maybe I'll find out what those "arrangements" are, he thought, opening his book. *I might even find a way to get Father to stop working with Lum. I don't care how much money we make. I sure don't like this. Not one bit.*

SIXTEEN

THE NEXT DAY, Jessamyn grabbed Cap's sleeve when he arrived at school.

"Mr. Jones is coming this afternoon to fix a hole in the floor," she told him with shining eyes. "If you come with me after school, we could spy on him."

Cap was only too happy to agree.

He hurried home for his dinner at the noon break. Voices sounded from the parlor, so he crept into the warm kitchen.

Blast! he thought. *Another literary meeting!* At least Mamma couldn't ask him to recite, for he had school. It was time for his dinner, anyway. As if on cue, his stomach growled. The steaming kitchen smelled sweetly of cloves and Cap's mouth watered. But to his surprise, no plate waited for him upon the checked tablecloth.

"There you are," Mrs. Hardy said, sweeping into the room.

"Mrs. Hardy, where's my—"

"*She's* here again," the housekeeper said at the same moment, busily slicing her warm raisin cake, "and she's brought that girl of hers with her. As though I didn't have enough work to do, I must wait on those two as well."

"Oh," Cap said, eyeing the rest of the cake on the sideboard. "Well, I'll just take some cake and go back to school." But Mrs. Hardy slapped his hand away as he reached for the dessert.

"Your mother wants you in the parlor," she said shortly. "Go."

With dragging steps, Cap went, but the room wasn't filled with ladies holding teacups, chatting and laughing over books.

"Why, hello," Delphia said, beaming at him from her perch on their threadbare sofa. Jardine nodded at him from nearby, holding a volume of poetry. And Dr. Ivins was chatting with Mamma, seated in her favorite easy chair by the window. Mrs. Hardy swept into the room, grimly carrying the tray laden with cups of tea and slices of cake.

"Here," she said shortly, setting the tray none too gently upon a side table. With that, she turned and swept from the room.

Mamma blinked but recovered quickly, smiling at her guests and making to rise from her chair so she could serve them herself.

"I'll do that, Mamma," Cap quickly said. He brought everyone a cup of tea and handed round the cake. Mamma beamed and Dr. Ivins smiled his approval.

"Good lad," he said. "Make yourself useful to your mother. She needs to avoid straining herself."

Cap sat gingerly on the edge of the sofa near Delphia and picked up his own slice of cake with his fingers, taking a large bite. When Mamma narrowed her eyes, he dropped the cake and picked up his fork, ducking his head.

Delphia giggled. "I think you have more books than the library, Mrs. Cooper," she said. "I surely admire that."

"Thank you," Mamma said, while a faint flush brightened her cheeks. "Now, how are your studies?" she asked Delphia, taking a tiny sip of her tea. "Your mother tells me you plan to apply to a medical college soon." Her brow crinkled slightly as Delphia nodded. "I didn't know there were any medical schools in this country that accepted ladies," Mamma added.

"There is one, now," Delphia said eagerly. "The college in Philadelphia, the city I was named after, is allowing women to study medicine. I aim to be one of their first students. I surely hope they'll consider me," she said, while her brown skin flushed. "It's all I want in this world." She glanced down and picked up her fork.

Dr. Ivins cleared his throat. "That reminds me," he said, placing his cake plate back on the tray. "My assistant spoke to me a while ago, asking for my help in this matter."

Jardine drew in a breath, while Delphia paused with a bite of cake halfway to her mouth. Dr. Ivins drew an envelope from his waistcoat pocket. "I believe that this letter of introduction and recommendation might be of use to you, Delphia. I am honored to recommend you to a professor who teaches at that medical college. He is a former colleague of mine from my days in New York."

The man handed the envelope to Delphia, who was speechless for once. Her face glowed like a Christmas tree lit with hundreds of candles.

"Oh, Dr. Ivins," Jardine said. Her eyes filled with tears. "How can we ever..." Her voice caught and she pulled out a handkerchief.

Dr. Ivins cleared his throat again, but he was clearly pleased. "Think nothing of it. Jardine, you've been the most able assistant I've ever had, and your daughter belongs in medicine. She's a star pupil, with a mind like a steel trap. She put the students who attended my last anatomy lecture to shame, every one of them."

Anatomy lecture. Cap chewed slowly while ruminating on the strangeness of the situation. Here he was, sitting all civilized and polite, eating cake with ladies who didn't know he had helped dig up their neighbors to sell to medical schools. Of course, Delphia had only mentioned seeing drawings at the latest lecture, but once she got to medical school, there would be corpses all ready to cut up.

She's got to know that at least some of them were snatched by people like Lum, Cap told himself, quietly glancing at the girl next to him. Delphia had put her cake aside and was reading her letter with shining eyes. The sight made Cap's stomach twist. Whether or not Delphia knew where all the cadavers came from, her joyful face filled his heart with guilt that weighed heavy as iron.

What would they all think of me? he asked himself. *What would Mamma think?* His cake turned to ash in his mouth. Gulping his tea, Cap rose to his feet. As he did so, he knocked against the satchel Delphia had set down, and a folded paper fell from the open flap. The girl's eyes widened.

"I almost forgot," she said. She snatched the paper from the floor and handed it to Dr. Ivins. As he read, she told the others about seeking signatures from the townspeople to ask for a watch at the cemetery. "I hate to impose again, sir, after all you've done for me, but would you consider signing my letter?"

Quickly gathering plates and cups, Cap piled them onto the tray and hurried to the door. He could hardly stand being in that room any longer. The fire had grown uncomfortably hot, and his thoughts had grown so prickly and sharp it hurt to think.

Mamma nodded at him, and Cap turned to go. Then, the doctor's words halted his steps.

"I'm certain you are aware, Delphia, that medical schools need subjects for dissection. Given our town's recent events, I'm sure it's been on your mind. Of course, there are...different methods for obtaining them. Methods that are less distasteful, if you will."

"Exactly," Delphia said. "Schools must get their subjects legally. They should never buy them from those awful, ghoulish robbers. I aim to protect my friends and family. Please sign this, sir."

"I am happy to do so," the doctor said gravely.

Hunching his shoulders, Cap returned to the kitchen, snatched his coat, and fled.

SEVENTEEN

UNABLE TO CONCENTRATE, Cap spent a miserable afternoon at school, watching several girls pass notes to one another while a boy named Jasper picked his nose repeatedly. The large clock on the teacher's desk seemed frozen. Cap slumped in relief when Master Rankin signaled the end of class.

The moment the teacher let them go, Jessamyn snatched her things from her desk and hurried to the cloakroom. She didn't spare him a glance in passing, but Cap figured she didn't want to attract too much attention from the others. After all, many of their classmates had taken to snickering and whispering each time the two spoke.

He stopped short once he reached the cloakroom. Jessamyn was nowhere in sight.

Grabbing his things, Cap trotted outside. He could just spot Jessamyn at the end of the block, walking fast with her head down. Struggling into his coat, Cap felt something inside one of the pockets. He pulled out a tiny slip of paper. Unfolding it, he read:

I have to go home. Please don't come.

Jessamyn

Jamming the paper back into his pocket, Cap watched as the girl disappeared from his sight.

"Aw, shucks, did your girl leave you?" Eli taunted, coming up from behind. He elbowed Cap as he passed. "Guess she doesn't like you after all. 'Course, we all know why you like *her*," he said, running off to join his friends.

The other boys laughed as Cap turned to face them, scowling. His hands clenched into fists, and he had half a mind to finally make good his threat to punch Eli's mean-talking mouth. But picturing Mamma's scandalized face and Father's punishment, he reconsidered.

Gulping air, he turned his back and started running after Jessamyn. She owed him an explanation, and he was determined to have one.

He ran several blocks and finally stopped for a breather near the mayor's office when someone bumped him so hard, he fell over onto the frozen earth.

"Watch your step!" Cap said, dusting off his trousers.

"You watch your tongue, boy, or I'll cut it right out of your mouth," a man growled. Cap looked up into the bleary eyes of Dr.

Rusch, the very man who had declared Jessamyn dead. The doctor turned away and walked on without a backward glance.

Dr. Rusch or Jessamyn? Cap asked himself, bouncing on his feet. He surely wanted to speak to Jessamyn and discover why she'd ditched him, but curiosity over the strange events that had led to the girl's miraculous revival won out.

I'll talk to her later, he vowed to himself, trotting after the doctor. *This doctor has something to do with Lum's business, I'm sure of it.*

They walked for several blocks, the doctor striding along at a fast pace and the boy creeping behind with a hammering heart. When the doctor left the downtown area and marched directly to the Round House, Cap stopped short and barely avoided exclaiming out loud.

A new sign hung above the front door: "Circleville College of Medicine." Workers were busy painting window and door frames, while others carried lumber and tools.

That's why the bodies we dig up don't go to Columbus—they stay right here! Cap thought with a sickening jolt to his stomach. He shook his head in disbelief. As soon as people knew about the place, wouldn't they be banging on the doors, demanding to see if the missing bodies were there?

Dr. Rusch entered the red brick building with a jaunty step. Cap hung back until the man was out of sight. He didn't dare follow through the main doors, but cut around to the back. Soon, he came upon a tiny window at ground level. He tried the latch, which opened quite obligingly with a soft squeak.

Carefully, he peered inside. All was dark and silent. Cap crouched down and managed to work his legs through the opening. He took a deep breath, steeled himself for the plunge, and then froze as a hand seized his leg.

He screamed as he was pulled roughly into the room, landing on the floor in a heap.

"I'll fix your flint, you guttersnipe!" a man bellowed. "Thought you'd spy on us, didn't you? Want to see the blood, eh, boy?"

"No," Cap gasped and scrambled away.

The man who'd seized Cap held a lantern high as he studied the boy with narrowed eyes. He was thin and bent and his pallid face was rough as leather.

"Well, we just might find a use for you," he said. The skin of his face crinkled as his thin lips cracked into a wide smile. "We could use a boy around here to pick up the spare arms and legs. What do you say to that?"

"Leave him be, Parsons," another man said from the doorway. The speaker, a pudgy man with sparse blond hair, hurried inside. "I wager he'll not be the last lad to steal into the dissection room looking for a thrill."

Dissection room? Cap gulped and looked about him. The wedge-shaped room was cold and damp, with stone walls and floor. In the center stood a long table with a bucket beneath it. A smaller table stood against the wall, with a cluttered assortment of metal tools. One was a large saw with glinting, jagged teeth. He swallowed again.

"And, now, young man, you will leave through the front door like a gentleman," the stout man said. He didn't wait for an answer. He simply took Cap's arm with a firm grip and led him from the room.

Without a word, Cap allowed himself to be shown outside. The moment the door closed in his face, he grinned and walked down the steps. Then, he sprinted back around the building to the tiny window and peeked inside. A lantern glowed from the small table, but Parsons was nowhere in sight.

Before he could change his mind or lose his nerve, Cap drove his legs through the open window and dropped to the cold stone floor. He yelped when he realized he wasn't alone. A figure now lay on the long table, covered with a smudged white sheet.

Footsteps and voices sounded from above and were moving closer. Cap sped back to the window, but it was high enough that he could not easily climb back outside. He looked about frantically. What could he do? They were almost at the door!

Not one of the medical students noticed that the sheet covering the corpse fluttered a bit, almost as if something had disturbed it. They crowded into the room, talking, laughing, and smoking the same foul tobacco Father often enjoyed.

Cap crouched beneath the table, surrounded by feet on all sides, hugging his knees to his chest. There was no escape.

Now, why did I have to do such a blamed fool thing? he asked himself.

Voices in the room grew silent as one man spoke. There was no mistaking the reedy voice of Dr. Rusch.

"Gentleman, shall we proceed?" Dr. Rusch asked. "Reeves, Carter, you shall assist." Feet shuffled and changed places. Several of the students gasped as part of the sheet was pulled down.

"You see the red tissue here that protrudes from between the eyelids? This is a 'conjunctival tumor.' Carter? My pointer,

please. Reeves, shift him over a bit so your fellow students can
see better."

As Dr. Rusch lectured, a student shoved the body to the side of
the table. The corpse's arm slid off the edge and swung gently for
a moment, inches from Cap's nose. Without thinking, Cap reached
out to swat the cold, dark-skinned limb away from his face.

"Aaaaugh!" a voice bellowed above Cap's head. The room exploded into chaos, and feet scrambled away from the table. Tripping over one another, several students fled the room, shouting
and swearing.

"My eye! My eye!" the voice cried. "It hurts! What are you doing to me, doctor?"

Holding his breath, the boy watched as the formerly lifeless
arm moved in front of his nose. Fingers flexed, a fist clenched,
and the arm rose out of sight.

"Here, now, Mr., uh…" Dr. Rusch spluttered.

"Johnson," the man said. "Where am I?"

"Here, sir, let us help you down," the doctor said. "We were
treating your eye in our, eh, operating room. We meant to remove
the tumor, but must not have given you enough ether to keep you
asleep. Come, sir, we'll help you to your room."

"This ain't the hospital," Mr. Johnson said. "Where am I?"

The man's bare feet reached the floor, and someone pulled the
sheet from the table and wrapped it about the reanimated corpse.
Cap inched backward, away from the retreating feet of Dr. Rusch,
who helped the man from the room.

Sitting cross-legged on the stone floor, he ran a hand through
his tangled hair and tried to breathe.

"Sakes alive," Cap whispered. "It's real. That power, it's real!"

He sat in the cold, silent room for a while, hugging his knees and grinning to himself. If he could help Mamma and her new baby, well, that made joining Lum's business worth its while, by golly.

Quickly sobering, Cap got to his feet. It may have been worth working with Lum just to have the chance to revive Jessamyn and those other folks, but that didn't mean Cap had to stay in the business. That was for sure.

As he carefully climbed the stairs, wary of the noise coming from other places in the building, Cap remembered Dr. Ivins's words. "There are different methods for obtaining" subjects for dissection, he'd said. "Methods that are less distasteful." What did he mean by that? Could there be a way to provide bodies for medical schools that didn't involve secretly digging up one's friends in the dark of night?

With a jolt, Cap stopped short. The arrangement! The sexton had mentioned it, outside the grand yellow house. If there was some kind of arrangement, why didn't the doctors use that method, instead of buying bodies dug up in secret?

I'll ask Dr. Ivins, Cap promised himself. *He'll know.* The thought alone sent a rush of energy and a lightened sense of hope all through his body.

Perhaps Father and I can finally leave this devilish business. It's getting too risky anyway—with a medical college right in our town, that's the first place people will look for the bodies.

EIGHTEEN

WHEN HE REACHED the top of the stairs, rapid footsteps and the swish of skirts headed in his direction. Cap spied a narrow door and darted inside a broom cupboard that smelled of mice. He pulled the door closed and held his breath. The footsteps approached, the knob rattled, and the door swung open.

"Cap Cooper? What on earth are you doing here?" Jardine asked him, holding a candle high as she studied his face.

"I, uh," the boy said, blinking and squinting at the light. "I don't know," he finally said.

"You don't know?" the woman said, staring down at Cap with a furrowed brow. She placed her hands on her hips.

"I was passing by, is all," Cap said, "and I thought I'd take a look inside. A medical college. Golly." Even Cap knew how silly his flimsy excuse sounded.

Jardine surprised him by laughing out loud. "And you thought you'd explore the college's fine broom cupboard," she said, wiping her eyes.

"I heard someone coming and didn't want to get caught," Cap said, truthfully enough.

Jardine shook her head at him, but she was smiling. "You shouldn't be here. I'll see you out, but first I need to pick up some books for my daughter. Come along."

Biting his lip, Cap followed her to a wide spiral staircase. No one else seemed to be around the place, thankfully. They climbed in silence to a narrow landing, then climbed another set of steps to the third floor. Jardine fished a key from her pocket, unlocked the door, and led the boy inside.

He gasped at the sight that met him. Shelves climbed to the ceiling, holding dozens of thick books. A massive desk stood in one corner.

"It sure took us a long while to move all this into the doctor's new office," Jardine said. "But he's right pleased with it."

A portrait of Dr. Ivins hung above a small fireplace. In the painting, the doctor's arm was around a raven-haired woman. A young girl with a long, black braid over her shoulder sat in front of the couple. She smiled down at a brindled cat in her arms.

"I didn't know Dr. Ivins had a family," Cap said.

Jardine moved to stand beside him. "His wife and daughter died many years ago. It like to tore the man up inside. That's why he works so much. He wants to save folks so their families don't have to grieve the way he does."

"Oh," Cap said. His mind immediately flew to the new illness Dr. Ivins had warned him of. "He told me of the strange fever that's going around. Is that how they died?"

Jardine crossed her arms as she studied the portrait. "I don't know," she admitted. "All I know is Dr. Ivins came here to get a fresh start." She smiled at Cap. "And I'm so glad he did. He gave me a job when others closed the door in my face, and he treats anyone who comes to him. Besides, he's the best doctor around. Everybody says so."

"Well, will Dr. Ivins be by, soon?" Cap asked, itching to talk to the man.

Shaking her head, Jardine took two books from the doctor's desk and shooed Cap toward the door. "No. He's off caring for another poor soul who took sick. Well, let's go," she said.

"Yes, ma'am," Cap said, as the woman locked the door behind them. They quickly descended the stairs and headed outside.

The sky was clouding over and the streetlamps were already on when they reached the street outside. Just then a group of workmen came from around the side of the house, carrying tools and boards. With them was Lum, who bellowed out a loud laugh. His mirth died away at the sight of Cap and the woman. With a scowl and a muttered oath, he turned on his heel and marched off in the opposite direction.

"Come, I'll walk you home," Jardine said to Cap, as she watched the man leave.

"No, thank you, ma'am," Cap said. "I'm going to see a friend. I can get home by myself."

"You sure?" Jardine asked, still watching Lum as he swiveled around a corner and out of sight.

"Yes," Cap said. Jardine's strange reaction at hearing Lum's name the other night came to mind. Clearing his throat, Cap asked: "Do you know who that fellow was?"

Jardine turned sharply to look Cap in the eye. "I believe that's Columbus Jones, who works with your father."

Nodding, Cap remained silent.

With a sigh, Jardine regarded Cap for a moment in silence. Finally, she spoke.

"I don't mean to talk disrespectfully of anyone, but I believe you should steer clear of that man. I have it on good faith that he might be tied up in the grave robbing. We don't know for certain, but my husband is mighty suspicious, and so am I."

Cap nodded, unable to speak. Jardine smiled at him.

"I didn't say this to scare you none, child. I only want you to be careful around that old Mr. Jones. Maybe you could let your father know."

Nodding again, Cap turned to go, waving goodbye to the woman. She smiled at him, and he did his best to smile back.

What would she say if she knew Father and I have been working for Lum? he thought.

NINETEEN

TURNING HIS STEPS to St. Joseph's, Cap hurried along, hoping Jessamyn would talk to him. He couldn't understand what had made her change her plans and head home without a word. He fingered the crumpled note inside his pocket and frowned. Surely, it was some kind of misunderstanding.

He hurried past the line of oak trees that stood like a row of old, bowed soldiers outside the orphanage, approached the door and knocked. The Sister who answered squinted at him from behind wire-rimmed glasses.

"I came to see Jessamyn," he said.

The woman stared at him for a moment. "Wait here," she said.

Stomping his feet and trying to keep warm, Cap waited several slow minutes until the door finally opened again.

"She's not here," the woman told him shortly, before shutting the door in his face.

Cap shoved his hands into his pockets and glowered. Where else would the girl be? He didn't believe that old lady at all.

I'm not leaving without talking to her, he vowed to himself. *No, sir!* And after only a few minutes, he had what he needed and headed to the back door of the orphanage.

"Coal for the kitchen," he told the elderly Sister who answered his knock. He carried a rusted bucket filled with coal scavenged from the ground nearby.

"This way," the woman muttered. If she was surprised that someone was delivering coal this time of the evening, she didn't show it. Cap followed her to the kitchen and placed the bucket near the box by the massive black stove.

"I'll unload this and let myself out, ma'am," he said.

The Sister shrugged and limped away. "Thank you, child."

Left alone, Cap dumped the coal and crept toward the hall that led upstairs. Hardly breathing, he tiptoed up the staircase. He clung to the shadows of the dimly lit hallway, relieved to find that Jessamyn's door was open, and then startled at the voices coming from inside.

"It is a miracle, indeed," Dr. Rusch was saying. "I saw you pass from this world, child. We all grieved so at the loss."

So, she is here, Cap thought. His insides smarted. Why didn't she want to see him? And why was that old Dr. Rusch here, again, when nobody liked him?

"But how did she get out of that coffin? The sexton vowed that he buried her." Sister Mariah's throaty voice was unmistakable.

Fighting the urge to flee, Cap stood his ground, heart in his throat.

"I believe we'll have answers in time," Dr. Rusch said in a rapid voice, "but let's not speak of this, now. My concern is for the dear girl, who so recently—"

"Where is Dr. Ivins?" Sister Mariah cut in. "I was told he would be here."

"He's busy," Dr. Rusch snapped.

"I see," Sister Mariah said after a moment.

Cap listened as the doctor asked about a hundred questions. He pressed Jessamyn to try to remember her illness, and what had happened when she was found and brought back home.

The man *had* to be Lum's contact. Cap was certain of it. He swallowed as fear coated his insides with a winter chill. Dr. Rusch had paid Lum for an undelivered body, but why? To cover his own tracks?

Mouth dry, the boy began to edge away. This wasn't going as planned, and he did not fancy being so close to Dr. Rusch. He'd try to talk to Jessamyn another time.

As Cap turned, his foot kicked the dustpan that someone had left near the top of the stairs. It clattered and clanged all the way to the floor below until it finally came to a rest, spinning on the cracked tiles like a child's toy top.

He bolted away from the stairs and the commotion of voices in Jessamyn's room, through the long shadows of the corridor. As he passed a window, weak moonlight showed him the outline of a door opposite the glass. He turned mid-stride and seized the handle. Mercifully, it was unlocked. He wrenched the door open, hurtled inside, and turned to close the door as quietly as possible.

"Who is it?" a woman asked.

Yelping, Cap turned as someone lit a candle. He was in a bedroom, spare and small as Jessamyn's, with only a bed, a table, and a wooden chair. A woman sat up in the bed, staring at Cap. Tawny hair cascaded down her shoulders in loose curls, and there was something familiar about her face.

"I, uh, I'm sorry, ma'am," Cap said, gasping the words out. "I didn't know this was your room."

"That's all right, young man, but you look as if you're being chased by the devil himself," the woman said with a small grin.

"He could be," Cap said. He turned to open the door, but froze. Footsteps hurried up and down the hall, and voices chattered. Cap turned back and searched for a window. There wasn't one.

The woman placed the candle on the table. "Sit down, child, if you're going to stay."

Cap's face burned. He shouldn't be here, alone in the bedroom of one of the Sisters, but what else could he do? He sat on the single chair in the room, struggling to breathe. He'd wait a few minutes until the furor died down before trying to sneak out.

"I'm sorry, Sister, I'll leave as soon as I catch my breath," he huffed, straining to listen to the commotion outside.

"That's all right, young man. I don't often get visitors. And you don't have to call me 'Sister,' I'm not one of the nuns here." The woman smiled and Cap gaped. He knew why she looked so familiar. Though her hair was different, the curve of her cheek and the shape of her nose and lips were well known to Cap. He'd spent plenty of time at school gazing at a similar face.

"Jessamyn!" Cap blurted before he could stop himself. "You look like Jessamyn!"

TWENTY

THE WOMAN LAUGHED. One of her caninc teeth was missing. "I've never heard anyone say that before. Usually they say my daughter looks like me."

Cap stared in shock. Jessamyn wasn't an orphan?

"How do you know my daughter?" the woman asked, her pale face alight.

"School," Cap replied, plucking at his collar.

"Oh, of course," the woman said. The skin beneath the woman's eyes was smudged purple. One eyelid was badly swollen and oozed a thick, yellow liquid. Cap winced at the sight of it.

"I didn't know Jessamyn had a mother," he said.

"Most people do not," the woman said, looking away to a spot somewhere above Cap's head. Her eyes were full of sadness. Cap backed up another step, while many new questions tumbled about in his head.

Someone knocked.

"Hide," the woman whispered, nodding at the corner behind the door. Cap darted to the corner just in time for the wooden door to creak open and conceal him from sight.

Dr. Rusch swept in and deposited his bag on the table. Cap listened with a hand clapped over his mouth.

"And how are you, today, Tillie?" Dr. Rusch said. Bottles clinked as the man rummaged about in his bag.

"Well enough, thank you," Tillie answered in a soft voice.

"Take this," the doctor said, while pouring something into a cup.

"What is it?" Tillie asked.

The doctor didn't answer. More bottles clinked together. Then Dr. Rusch cleared his throat. "Jessamyn is doing well," he said, "but I must remind you not to see her. You don't want her to catch your illness."

"But—"

"I'll return next week," Doctor Rusch said, cutting her off. He began to sweep bottles back into his bag.

"But what of my eye, Doctor?" Tillie said.

"Ah, yes," Dr. Rusch said. "Most interesting, I must say. Why, I was just looking at a similar case this morning. Fellow had a tumor the size of a swallow's egg in his left eye. We were not able to remove it, I'm afraid. He died just before we could operate."

Cap's hands turned to ice. Mr. Johnson, the man he'd revived on the dissection table, was dead again. What had happened to him?

"Oh, the poor man," Tillie murmured.

"Now, don't you fret over it. I shall be able to study his tumor and perhaps it will be to your good." The doctor moved toward the door. "I may learn what to do for others who suffer from similar conditions. We shall advance the great cause of science, that man and I!"

He swept from the room and pulled the door closed behind him.

Cap didn't know what to say. He waited. Finally, Tillie glanced in his direction.

"You should go, young man. Careful no one sees you leave my room. It's not proper for you to be here."

The boy nodded. He cracked the door open to listen for any sound. There was none, so he whispered goodbye to Jessamyn's mother and crept out into the now deserted corridor and down the stairs.

Cap made it to the cabbage-reeking kitchen. Finding it empty, he crouched by the fire. His head whirled.

Jessamyn and her mother lived together at St. Joseph's? It made no sense. He leaned forward and held cold hands closer to the crackling flames. Why didn't Jessamyn tell everyone she wasn't an orphan?

"Why, this is a surprise," Sister Mariah said. Cap leapt at the sound and knocked over the heavy iron poker. It fell to the stone floor with a *clang*.

"Goodness, child, you're as jumpy as a mouse in a hot skillet," Sister Mariah said with a chuckle. She picked up the poker and returned it to the hearth. Cap was certain his face was as red as the glowing coals behind him.

"I came to see Jessamyn," he said.

"Captain Cooper, I assumed as much, but the child isn't feeling well and it's late. I must ask you to return tomorrow."

"She's not feeling well?" he asked.

Sister Mariah's face was troubled. "She seemed feverish when she came home, so I called for the doctor."

I know, Cap thought. *She called Dr. Ivins, but Rusch came instead.*

Something wasn't right. Could it be that Dr. Rusch was somehow making patients *worse*, rather than better? Cap wasn't sure of much, but he knew he didn't trust old Dr. Rusch, with his squashed pumpkin nose and his sneering face, not one little bit.

"Can't I just see her for one minute?" he begged.

The woman smiled at him, but she took his arm in her firm grip and steered him to the door. "She'll be fine," she said. "I plan to keep an eye on her myself."

"But—"

"Go," Sister Mariah said, turning the knob. "She'll be all right, I promise. But you might say a prayer or two for your friend."

"Like God ever listens to *me*," Cap muttered, buttoning his coat.

Sister Mariah folded her arms, regarding Cap with a sad expression. She placed a gentle hand on his shoulder.

"He does listen, child," she told him in a soft voice. "But he may not answer in the way you expect. I once asked for the means to help children like your friend Jessamyn. So many have no place to call home. And I got what I asked for in a way I never could have imagined."

"You did?" Cap asked.

"Yes," the woman answered. Her eyes sought and held Cap's. "And I believe you understand what I'm saying. Don't you?"

Cap shrugged, while chills crept up his spine. "No, ma'am. I can't say I do."

Sister Mariah blinked. Then, she straightened and spoke in a brisk voice. "Cap, you'd best skedaddle," she said. "Your parents would settle my hash if they knew I was keeping you here, making you late for your supper."

When he got home, no one scolded Cap for being late, for no one was about. Mamma was sleeping, Mrs. Hardy was gone, and Father was who knew where. Cap ate the plate of food kept warm on the stove, wondering just how much Sister Mariah knew about him.

It doesn't matter, he thought as he gulped his beans and bread. *I'm going to raise every last soul they tell us to dig up. No more money for old Lum. No more money for Dr. Rusch. I'm done doing their dirty work.*

When Father came in, telling Cap he had a job to do with Lum, the boy smiled.

"Yes, sir," he said.

TWENTY-ONE

"**Y**OU COULDA KNOCKED me over with a feather when I heard we had us another easy job!" Lum said. "This is the life for me, boy! He pays them, you know," he said, leaning down to whisper. "He pays them so's they'll let us take 'em when they're dead."

The arrangement! Cap's pulse quickened. "Who pays them?" he asked.

"No questions, boy," Lum growled. He continued to drive, flicking the reins of Father's wagon and whistling to Hilda. "Just do your job and get paid. Our man pays them folks as he knows they're dying, to let us take them. 'For the advancement of science,' he always tells them, though most of them takes the money 'cause their families need it. Don't know why *this* fella needs more coin, but you never know. Could've lost all his living at the horse races."

Lum's words were eerily familiar. No more than an hour ago, Dr. Rusch had said nearly the same thing to Tillie, while Cap hid behind the door. His chest grew tight, and he clenched his fists.

Dr. Rusch thinks he's so smart, but he's sure in for a surprise. He's not getting any more bodies from Lum.

As the wagon rumbled along in the darkness, Cap shivered and wrapped his arms around his quivering frame. It still made no sense that the doctor had paid them for Jessamyn. Dr. Rusch might have paid Lum because he didn't want anyone asking questions, but what did the man have to hide? Aside from his resurrection business, that is.

"We're here," Lum whispered as he jerked on the reins and pulled the wagon to a stop. "The father's waiting for us."

They parked beside a tall brick house with shuttered windows. A thin man waited for them beside the door. Deep smudges of purple beneath the man's bloodshot eyes stood out against his light, papery skin. Wordlessly, he led them inside a laundry room where basins lined the wall.

"Wait here," the man whispered before he disappeared. Within moments, he returned, carrying a bundle wrapped tightly in a colored cloth. It was a child, no more than half Cap's height by the looks of the swaddled form. Cap's eyes grew wide with horror.

"My wife does not know about this," the man whispered. "Please, go quickly."

"Yes, sir," Lum said, saluting smartly. When he reached to seize the bundle, Cap stepped in front of him.

"I'll take him," he said. The man glanced down in surprise but didn't protest. Cap balanced the bundle in his arms. The body felt light, hardly more than the weight of a puppy. He turned to go, following Lum out the door, but a sudden heaviness was settling inside his chest. He couldn't breathe. He had to say something.

"Why?" Cap asked, turning back. "Why are you letting us take him?"

The man gazed at Cap with a pleading expression.

"So that the doctors might discover why he was…the way he was," he said, his face twisted in grief. "So that perhaps one day they may know how to cure others like him."

"Move, boy," Lum hissed from the doorway.

Cap backed up a few feet, still staring at the man.

"But this is your son," he whispered.

"Go now!" the man said, his face crumpled. "Please!"

Crossing the kitchen in a few long strides, Lum snatched the bundle from Cap's arms and seized him by the wrist. He dragged him out into the cold night air. Then he tossed the small body into the back of the wagon, and hefted Cap in after it. The fabric of Cap's trousers tore over one knee when he landed.

Lum drove away like the flames of hell were at their heels. Cap and the small bundle were both thrown back and forth in the bed of the wagon like two potatoes in a wheelbarrow.

"Confound you, boy! Don't you ever pull a trick like that again!" Lum bellowed when they were a short distance from the house. "You'll lose us our money, you sniveling brat! 'But this is your son,'" Lum imitated in a high-pitched wail. "So what! You think your pa would never let them doctors have a go at you? You just wait 'til I tell Noah. He'll do you in himself and sell you to the highest bidder."

Cap struggled to keep his balance inside the jouncing wagon. Rage clouded his vision. He'd fix old Lum, for sure! Cap reached for the bundle and unwrapped the tightly wound fabric. As he did so, a lightness swelled inside his chest. *Here I go.*

When the final layer of fabric fell away, Cap blinked in surprise. In the moonlight, the boy's face was distorted, with eyes far too large for his face, a tiny, flat nose, and a gaping mouth. There was a strange ring of marks across the child's forehead, like a series of bruises.

He placed his hand on the child's cheek. The flesh was hard and cold as stone. Cap waited, not breathing, fully expecting the sensation of warmth to spark beneath his fingers and spread through the cold flesh of the dead child. The wagon jostled as they moved onto a cobbled street. Cap stared, waiting.

Nothing happened.

He waited for several more heart beats. He placed both hands on the child's face. *Please*, he silently prayed. More long moments passed. Cap felt his insides turn to lead.

It didn't work.

Slumping in defeat, Cap covered the child's face again. He couldn't even begin to understand all of this. He'd revived Jessamyn, Mr. Greeves, and Mr. Johnson, yet he was not able to revive the child beside him. Why?

Once the body was delivered, Lum took his payment with a smirk. He tipped his hat and sauntered off down the alleyway, leaving Cap to drive home on his own.

Cap felt in his pocket for the gold coin he still carried. He fished it out and hurled it as far as he could into the thick shadows. It landed somewhere with a metallic *ping* and rolled to a stop. And Cap drove away.

TWENTY-TWO

**GANG OF GHOULS
STRIKES AGAIN
IN FOREST
CEMETERY**

Excitement prevailing!

WHY COULDN'T I bring him back?

Sitting at his desk, Cap couldn't pay attention to his spelling book. That question kept coming back to sting him like a hornet with a powerful grudge.

Jessamyn wasn't in school. The troubling thought of what might be happening to her, well, that stung like a whole nest full of vengeful hornets. Cap fidgeted at his desk. If Jessamyn died again, he wasn't so certain he could revive her after all. He had to repeat several lessons and remain inside during afternoon recess, ciphering on his slate.

The evening wasn't much better. Mrs. Hardy served boiled cabbage for dinner, and there was no dessert. Then Father stopped him on the stairs.

"Lum spoke with me this morning," he said to Cap in a stern voice. "You tried to talk that man out of his arrangement."

"That was his *son*," Cap said, while the cabbage roiled uncomfortably in his stomach.

"It's no matter," Father said, his thick eyebrows meeting in the middle. "He agreed to it and was paid. Don't ask any more questions, and do your job. How many times must I tell you we need this money?" he said, taking his son's arm and giving it a little shake.

Wordlessly, Cap gazed up at his father. A cold lump settled inside his chest. "I'm sorry," he whispered.

"I know you don't like this work, and I admit it's distasteful, but those people are *dead*, Cap. We're not hurting them." Father's lips formed a thin line as he gazed at his son. "We've another digging job at the cemetery tonight, but Lum won't have you there. That means it'll take us much longer to do our work, and I'm tired enough as it is." Father ran a hand through his dark hair. "I'll speak to him tonight to see if I can get him to take you back." Without another word, his father left. And so, the dismal day ended.

The following morning, Cap sulked through school. Jessamyn had not yet returned. After class, he hurried into town, determined to see his friend.

As he passed Mr. Garrett's shop, the man waved him inside. Then he proudly displayed the invention Cap had helped him with. At the boy's suggestion, he'd added two more curved magnets to the electric charge-making device to get a stronger current. He'd also fashioned leather collars to which he'd attached the metal bits that needed to rest against the skin.

"This here's my second model," he said. "The man what ordered it already took the first one. He's mighty pleased with it. I sure do appreciate your help. You have a right quick mind, son."

"Thank you," Cap said, though the kind words couldn't quite lift his spirits.

Mr. Garrett mopped his sweaty forehead with a handkerchief and coughed out a wheezing bark.

"Papa, you're still coughing?" Lettie asked, coming in from the front shop. "Here, drink some water."

She handed her father a cup and then tossed a newspaper onto the table. "Special afternoon edition," she said. "I can't understand why anyone would do this. It's unnatural, that's what it is. Old Nellie's friends are carrying on like anything, and I can see why. I don't know what I'd do if that happened to you, Papa."

Mr. Garrett choked on his water. Spluttering, he wiped his mouth and patted his daughter's arm.

Cap glanced at the headline, and his insides froze.

Gang of Ghouls Strikes Again
in Forest Cemetery—Excitement Prevailing

He grabbed the paper and quickly read through the article. An elderly man, Wilson Jefferson, had died and been buried in a homemade coffin. Beside herself with grief, Wilson's wife, Alpharetta, jumped into the river the very next day. Friends opened the grave to bury Alpharetta with her husband, but found Wilson's body gone. A search was made of the town's new medical school, but nothing was found.

"Our town's fine colored residents now wonder where their loved ones lie," the article concluded. "A group, led by the Reverend Cole and his family, plans to meet before the courthouse today to ask for the town's protection and justice for the bereaved families."

"What did the paper say?" Mr. Garrett asked, squinting through his thick glasses. Cap told him, speaking in a rush as he buttoned his coat.

Mr. Garrett pursed his lips. "It's a shame, it is," he said, after a moment. "But I don't know what's to be done about it. Don't know at all." He began to cough again.

"You mind if I take this?" Cap asked, picking up the paper. Busy fussing over her father, Lettie nodded. Tying his scarf, Cap's thoughts whirled like a tornado. The snatchers couldn't have possibly guessed what would happen the very next day, after they stole Wilson's body. Well, Lum was sure in for it, now, with the town's residents in an uproar. It served him right.

Cap thanked Mr. Garrett and Lettie and left the shop. He couldn't go to the orphanage, now. He'd head home and show Father the paper. One way or another, he had to convince the man to give up the body-snatching business.

When he turned onto Main Street, Cap found himself part of a small crowd gathered in front of the courthouse. Their voices murmured in agreement and dismay as they listened to people speaking from the steps of the courthouse. Cap wove through and around the folks gathered there. With a fluttering heart, he recognized two of the people who were speaking. Delphia and Jardine stood side by side, along with several others, including a very tall man with brown skin who wore the collar of a preacher, and an elderly ebony-skinned man with bowed shoulders.

"My wife, Nellie, was stolen from her grave," the old man said. "And now they've taken others. We need a guard at the cemetery. Please."

"I have more than three hundred names who signed this letter," Delphia called out, proudly holding up her paper. "People all over town want to protect our loved ones. Please, listen to us!" She spied Cap and greeted him with a grateful smile.

Voices swelled and rose around her, as others called for action and help from the town. Cap backed away while his face burned with shame.

"Now, folks, I know you're upset, but there's no money available to pay a guard," someone else said. Cap recognized the mayor, a barrel of a man who bore a vivid wine-colored mark upon the pallid skin of his naked scalp. Voices called out in dismay.

"Then we must take matters into our own hands," Delphia called out. "Folks, listen to me! We'll organize our own watch if this town won't protect our loved ones. We'll catch those thieves and protect our own by ourselves!"

"I'll stand watch," a man yelled out. Gaping in shock, Cap watched as Parsons, the old man he'd met at the Round House, moved through the crowd, holding his hat in his hands and looking for all the world like a churchgoing soul who'd just been saved. "I sure don't like to see folks all in a dither, and this grave robbing don't set right with me," he said in a simpering voice. "I'm out of work and don't need much. If you all could give me what you could—some food, or maybe a penny or two, now and then, well…"

Cap gaped while the people on the steps spoke together excitedly, hurrying forward to shake Parsons's hand. That was the old man who had taunted him for climbing into the dissection room at the new medical college. Cap tilted his head. Had he been fired from the college? Then, a grating sound, like the crunch of gravel beneath his boot, caught his attention and he turned.

Lum was a few feet away, watching the gabbling crowd, snorting and chuckling with a look of delight on his florid face. Catching Cap's eye, he grinned and quickly winked one eye before he turned his back and walked away, whistling.

The mayor scratched at the mark on his head and eventually wandered off. Little by little, the crowd melted away after thanking Parsons for his Christian kindness. Grinning broadly, the skinny old man left, while people continued to pat him on the back as he walked. Delphia caught Cap's eye and waved, smiling broadly. Then she and her mother descended the steps and headed down the street with the tall preacher.

Cap swore his blood was bubbling like soup in a pot. Of all the nerve! With his mocking wink, Lum had let the cat out of the bag. Parsons was setting himself up to be a hero, pretending to watch over the town's dead, but he just happened to work for the doctor Cap was certain he was behind the body-snatching business. All he was doing was making sure a real guard wouldn't be there.

I've got to tell somebody what's going on, he decided. *No matter what Father thinks, we can't do this to our friends and neighbors. We shouldn't do this to anyone.*

TWENTY-THREE

"AH, THE WANDERER has returned," Mrs. Hardy said briskly as she swept inside and spied Cap slumped at the table. "I'd nearly forgotten what you looked like." The housekeeper tweaked his ear and began to rummage about in the cupboard, looking for something.

"Is Father here?" Cap asked. "I need to speak to him."

"No," Mrs. Hardy said. "And Mina is feeling poorly, again. I sent for the doctor, but your mother's *friend* came instead." The woman paused to glance down at the open newspaper in front of Cap. Wiping her hands on her apron, she read for a moment, then sniffed. "It says some of those folks plan to leave town. Good riddance, I say."

She slammed a floppy chicken down onto the table. At that moment, Jardine entered the kitchen. Her face was placid, so Cap thought perhaps she'd not overheard. Then, he saw the hurt in her eyes.

"Do you have any more ginger for tea...ma'am?" Jardine asked Mrs. Hardy in a controlled voice. Cap couldn't help noticing the slight pause before the word "ma'am." His heart leapt painfully inside.

Mrs. Hardy didn't turn around, but tore at the dead chicken while she spoke. "No, I do *not* have any more, you took it all. I could have used some when I visited Polly yesterday. That poor child couldn't even hold down a sip of water!" The woman continued to pluck the chicken. Feathers flew.

Jardine closed her eyes for a moment. Her lips were compressed.

"I am sorry," she said. "But you know how sick Mina has been."

Mrs. Hardy whirled around. "Do you think I don't know that?" She shook the dead chicken in her hand. A few more feathers floated to the floor.

Jardine pivoted upon her heel and moved toward the door, muttering the words "be slow to anger" several times under her breath. At least, that's what it sounded like to Cap.

"I need to go to the market," Jardine said aloud when she reached the threshold. "Please tell your mamma, Cap, that I'll be back."

Guilt settled in the boy's chest like a hard lump of iron. The woman looked more than tired, like weariness was soaked clean through to her bones.

"I'll go to the market for ginger. Do you need anything else?" Cap said, leaping to his feet.

Jardine's eyes took on a glow. She blinked rapidly several times before she reached out to squeeze Cap's shoulders.

"Thank you," she said. "Ginger root, a penny's worth, is all I need."

Without looking at Mrs. Hardy, Jardine turned in the direction of Mamma's bedroom, her shoulders square and her head held high.

Cap didn't dare look at the housekeeper as he pulled on his coat. Her freezing silence chased him from the house. He darted through the front garden and vaulted over the gate.

"Cap?" Jardine called from the front door. "Wait a moment."

"Yes?" he called back.

"Could you stop by my house, too? It's right behind the Front Street grocer's, on Oak. Number 23."

"Sure," Cap said, pulling on his mittens. "But why?"

"I need more raspberry leaves. Philadelphia will fetch you some. You just tell her I sent you."

"Yes, ma'am," Cap answered.

Jardine's smile lit her tired face.

Shopping accomplished, Cap turned the corner of Front Street and headed down Oak. This neighborhood was the one where old Nellie Jackson had lived. Cap glanced about guiltily, as though the woman's husband might be somewhere nearby, staring at him.

Number 23 was a narrow, two-story house that had seen too few coats of paint in far too many years. When Cap knocked, the door squeaked open and Delphia appeared.

"Hello, Cap. You know, I still haven't found anything about folks coming back to life. Is that why you're here?" she asked with a grin. The girl wore a pair of tiny eyeglasses balanced on her nose.

"Your mother sent me for raspberry leaves," he said.

"Come on in."

Delphia ushered Cap inside a small front parlor. "I'll be right back," she said.

The boy tapped his feet as he waited. Timeworn furniture was scattered about the room and small framed photographs stood on the mantel. The very same newspaper Cap had just been reading was upon a chair. He glanced away.

Delphia returned and handed him a small packet wrapped in brown paper. Then she pointed to an open volume on a nearby table.

"You remember Dr. Ivins telling me there are ways to get bodies for medical schools besides grave robbing?" she asked.

Nodding, Cap busied himself with carefully tucking the packet of raspberry leaves into his pocket, while trying to ignore his stinging face.

"Dr. Ivins told me after his last anatomy lecture that all the subjects he dissected were legal. He gets them the right way." Delphia said.

Cap cleared his throat. "The *right* way?" he asked.

Delphia tapped her finger on the thick book open upon the table. "Laws have been passed in other states that unclaimed bodies can be sent to medical schools," she said. "No digging up folks at night on the sly. I think our state should have laws like that, don't you?"

Certain his guilt had to be written all over his face, Cap answered. "Well, sure."

"Why, Cap, your face is as pale as a cream cheese," Delphia said, removing her tiny glasses and grinning impishly at him. "Don't tell me all this talk of grave robbing gives you a fright."

"'Course not," the boy said, moving quickly to the door.

"Tell Mamma I'll be at the library, will you?" Delphia asked him.

Cap nodded as he stepped out onto the front porch. Delphia's eyes twinkled. "Land sakes, Cap, you look peaked," she said as she closed the door. "You'd best go on home and lie down."

Hurrying home, Cap prayed Father would be there. He couldn't stand keeping quiet anymore.

Mrs. Hardy met him at the door. Her face was pinched with worry. "Run to town and find Dr. Ivins. Jardine's baby is coming early."

TWENTY-FOUR

MRS. HARDY'S HOME was filled with the smell of dried herbs. Jars that held everything the woman used for her teas and remedies lined the long shelves. It was a pleasant, homey place, much like Cap's own kitchen, but he couldn't keep his feet from tapping a nervous rhythm on the floor beneath his chair.

Mrs. Hardy set a plate in front of him, but he pushed it away. "I'm not hungry," he mumbled.

"Moping will do you no good. Dr. Ivins will have everything sorted, you'll see," she said. "Eat." She shoved the plate back beneath Cap's nose. With a sigh, the boy lifted his spoon. The cornmeal mush with ham gravy stuck like glue to the roof of his mouth, and the hovering housekeeper made him even more jumpy than he already was.

"Mrs. Hardy, you help lots of ladies have babies. You could go help Dr. Ivins," he said. "I'll be fine here on my own."

Mrs. Hardy whirled. Bits of rubbery dough clung to her hands, like small white mushrooms had taken root. Cap sank down in his chair.

"*She* didn't want me there," the Irishwoman said. Her mouth was drawn into a thin line, but her eyes were overly bright.

"Oh," Cap said. The two gazed at each other for a moment, until the woman blinked and turned around. Mrs. Hardy pounded her dough again. Cap had barely forced in another mouthful when a sudden thought made him choke.

"Delphia! She doesn't know!" he said, coughing.

"Who?" Mrs. Hardy asked, but Cap was already out the door. Mrs. Hardy's shouted pleas faded away as he ran.

Jardine's house was silent. Cap spent a few frantic seconds pounding on the door before he remembered. The library—Delphia had said she'd be there!

Cap sprinted through the darkness toward the building in the heart of the town, but by the time he arrived, sweating and panting, that place was dark and silent as well.

Double blast, and curse it! Cap swore to himself. *Where is she?*

Dejected, he headed back the way he'd come. Many people were still out on the streets despite the late hour, especially in the town center where the taverns and inns stood. Cap passed the saloon where he'd first spied Dr. Rusch. Loud laughter burst out of the open doors. The boy glanced that way and then skidded to a stop.

There in the doorway was Jessamyn's mother. Instead of a plain nightgown, Tillie wore a peacock-blue dress covered with ruffles and ribbons. A patch covered her swollen eye, and she wasn't alone. She supported the weight of a man with a red, sweaty face, who draped an arm about her shoulders.

As the pair stepped over the threshold, Cap darted into the shadows of the empty lot next door.

"You make a fine pirate, my lady," the man slurred, as he lifted a cup in a toast while they stumbled along the uneven boards of the sidewalk, passing within a few feet of Cap. Tillie smiled up at the man.

The wind stirred and flung a cloud of dried leaves into the boy's face, but he hardly felt it. A thought began to crystallize inside him, cold and sharp like splinters of ice. He shivered. *This* was why Jessamyn didn't tell anyone about her mother. Whatever Tillie was doing, it sure didn't look respectable.

As the pair passed by Cap's hiding place, the man stumbled and nearly fell.

"Steady, Jeb! Hold on to me, I'll help you get home," Tillie said.

"Thank you kindly," the man said, "But my wife would likely object." He laughed.

"I object as well," another voice added. A short, wide form marched up to the staggering couple, illuminated by the light coming from the windows of the Court Street Hotel.

"Sister Mariah!" Tillie gasped.

"You go on home to your wife, sir, and may the Lord forgive you," Sister Mariah said, "as your wife likely will not." With surprising strength, the tiny woman seized the man's arm and propelled him into the street.

Mumbling to himself, the man melted into the shadows.

"Come, Tillie," Sister Mariah said.

"I was only out for a drink, Sister Mariah," Tillie said. She stood tall with her arms crossed, defiant in stance before the other woman, though her voice was soft.

"A drink?" the other woman answered. "For shame, Matilda! With your illness and all, to go out in the cold and return to this establishment, like a dog turning to its vomit. *For shame!*" Sister Mariah thundered.

"Please understand, Sister," Tillie said in a tight voice. She stepped closer with her hands outstretched. "My daughter and I must leave this place. I nearly lost her, but by some miracle Jessamyn was returned to me. The sickness is spreading. We must leave! How else can I earn what we need to get away from here?"

"You say this is for your daughter? That child deserves much more than this." Sister Mariah said.

Tillie stopped short. Her blue dress was bright, and her tawny hair gleamed in the light of the single streetlamp that glowed at the corner.

"Yes, she does, Sister Mariah," she said in a ragged voice. "She deserves a father, but God took him, didn't He? I couldn't even give my Jessie a roof over her head with the few dollars a month I earned sewing day after day until the light was gone and my head ached. No one would even have me as a servant in their home with a child of my own to care for, especially when they knew who her father was. So, I went out and did what I could to put food in my baby's mouth. If God will punish me for it, so be it. At least my child didn't starve!"

Cap's heart ached in his chest as he watched the two women. Father felt the same way about his work with Lum. He was doing something most folks would say was bad because he thought it was the best way to help his family.

Tillie stood with her head in her hands. Her shoulders heaved and her slight form shook like a leaf in the wind. Sister Mariah was still as one of the statues inside the chapel at St. Joseph's. Stone-like and unyielding, she stood with her hands planted on her hips, looking for all the world like a figure carved of granite. A few seconds ticked by until, suddenly, the statue moved.

"God forgive me," Sister Mariah said in a hoarse voice as she closed the distance between her and Tillie. She folded her arms about the trembling woman and, together, they wept.

"'First remove the beam from thine own eye,'" Sister Mariah sobbed. The two women moved together toward the old church.

Cap's throat grew tight, and he jammed his hands into his pockets as he walked away. He turned down Oak and headed for number 23. He'd try once more. This time, Delphia was home. Her eyes grew wide with fear as she listened, and she grabbed his arm. Together they ran.

Dr. Ivins was inside Cap's kitchen when they burst through the door. His face was a mask of weariness.

"I'm sorry," he said.

Delphia pushed past him and ran to find her mother. Cap sank into a kitchen chair. "Please, God," he whispered. But after that, he found no more words inside his heart.

TWENTY-FIVE

T HE NEXT EVENING, bells rang inside the tower of a small church on Front Street. Mourners filed in and sat on narrow wooden benches.

Jardine and her husband had invited the Coopers to the memorial service for their tiny son. Mamma was too tired out to go anywhere, and Mrs. Hardy stayed with her. But Cap and Father had washed and combed, and sat stiffly in their Sunday best on the hard seats.

A tiny wooden box had been placed on the altar, decorated with a single sprig of holly tied with a blue ribbon. Cap squirmed and loosened his collar. His newly scrubbed skin itched.

I'll make certain that little box stays in the ground, he swore to himself. Besides, surely this baby was too small. Nobody could possibly want him for a subject.

"Shove over, boy," growled a harsh voice. Lum scooted into the pew next to Father. His matted hair hung down in his eyes, and his jacket was crumpled and looked as if it had never been washed.

Cap's limbs grew suddenly heavy. "What's *he* doing here?" he whispered to Father, while a chilling dread began to seep into his chest.

"Tell your boy to keep his trap shut," Lum whispered to Father. He threw a furious glance at Cap before he bowed his head as they were asked to pray.

"Hold your peace, Cap," Father whispered from the corner of his mouth as they listened to the prayer.

"No," Cap muttered, anger rising and smoldering within. Not a soul was safe in this town. Not with Dr. Rusch buying the flesh of the dead. Blast it, Cap should have told somebody already. But he'd been so caught up in what had happened to Jardine, the thoughts had flown away.

The congregation began to sing.

> *Rock of ages, cleft for me*
> *Let me hide myself in thee...*

The voices filled the church from floor to rafters. Cap trembled. He was in a fix now, that was all-fired certain. But he would not allow Lum to take Jardine's baby. He'd kept his mouth shut too many times, and lots of innocent folks had suffered for it.

"I won't do it," he whispered. He elbowed his father. "We can't take him."

Father stared straight ahead, with his jaw set.

Could my tears forever flow
Could my zeal no respite know...

All around them, the voices swelled louder, reaching a cre-
scendo and drowning all other sound. Father leaned toward Lum
and muttered something in the man's ear, but Cap didn't catch a
word.

Rage caused the words to burst from his mouth: "Damnation!
What did you say to him?" Cap yelled.

The song had ended. Someone coughed. Cap turned to find all
eyes on him, the heads of most in the church swiveling around to
see what the commotion was.

"Let us pray," Reverend Cole said, his voice echoing in the
chapel. With a rustle of clothing, and more than one disapproving
look, the congregation turned back around.

The boy sank lower in his seat. He tried to ignore the men sitting next to him. Father kept his eyes ahead.

The service was quiet and simple. Reverend Cole spoke of the
goodness of God. "He loves each person and creature, even the
tiniest sparrow," he said.

Cap could have sworn a knife was splitting his chest open. He
had to stop this. If he could somehow get to that tiny coffin, well,
then what? What in tarnation could he do?

"Let us pray that God will speak peace unto our souls," Reverend Cole said. "Let us seek to hear His voice in our hearts, that we
may know His Grace."

Please, God! I never knew how to hear your voice, but I need to hear
it, now. Where are you?

But God was silent.

The congregation stood at the end of the service. Lum hurried from his seat after the final "amen" and disappeared. Father kept a firm grip on Cap's arm. The boy was forced to join the crowd that moved toward the front doors, inching along slower than molasses on a frigid day in January.

Reverend Cole, Jardine, and Delphia stood at the doors to thank those who had attended. Cap received a warm handshake from the Reverend, a tiny smile from Jardine, whose eyes were red and swollen, and a swift hug from Delphia.

I'm sorry. He couldn't say the words out loud.

When they finally reached the street, Lum was waiting for them. "Let's go," he hissed to Noah.

"I won't do it," Cap said with clenched teeth.

"Shut yer gob, boy!" he roared.

"Hold your tongue, Lum," Father said in a sharp voice. "You're speaking to my son."

"Your son is a lily-livered, no-good sack of horse manure!" Lum growled. "If'n you want him to be a partner, that boy's gotta learn to be a man. Right now, he's useless and spineless. I have half a mind to sell him to the doctors myself."

Father said nothing. Though he clenched his fists and narrowed his eyes, breathing hard, he did not speak.

Seconds passed. For Cap, the brief passage of time was a small eternity as he waited for Father to defend him against Lum's cruel words. But Father was silent. Cap felt as if the icy wind suddenly filled his body, freezing skin, flesh, and bone. He was cold as the bodies they plucked from their graves.

Then, Father glanced at him. "Leave us, Cap."

"That's right, boy," Lum said with a sneer, cuffing Cap hard on the ear.

"Leave him be," Father hissed. He held out his arm to block another blow Lum aimed in Cap's direction.

"Or you'll what?" Lum said, baring his teeth like a dog.

Father landed a blow to Lum's jaw that sent the older man staggering. He righted himself and plowed into Father, and the two fought, swearing and grunting. A small parcel dropped to the ground with a dull *thud*. Cap knew what it was. Lum had already done his job.

The boy stared for the space of a heartbeat, while rage spread like acid through his veins. Then, he moved. He darted closer, dodging Lum's flailing fists, seized the tiny cloth-wrapped bundle, and fled as though all the demons in hell were in pursuit.

TWENTY-SIX

C AP DIDN'T STOP until he reached home, certain his pursuer
would never believe he'd go there. Lum would surely think
he was heading to Jardine's home.

When he ducked beneath the willow tree, tips of the trailing
branches brushed through his hair as though trying to comfort
him. Gasping for air, he listened for signs of any pursuit. Once
certain there were none, he let himself into his workshop.

He lit his lantern and unwrapped the bundle. The baby reminded him of a child's toy. He could have easily held him in one
hand. Its tiny face was peaceful.

"Please, God, let it work now! I don't rightly know why I revived those first three people but not that boy, but now, please,
please, let this work," he whispered.

Cap hurriedly made the sign of the cross and muttered a quick prayer to Saint Anthony; patron saint of those who were lost. At least, that's what Mrs. Hardy had once said.

Whatever you do, please help me! Perhaps you're the one who can, he prayed.

Removing his gloves, he placed a hand on the baby's head, squeezed his eyes shut, and counted the seconds. An owl hooted from somewhere outside. Opening one eye, Cap stole a quick glance at the infant's face. No change. He closed his eyes and waited.

Seconds stretched out. Cap's feet were sore from running. His hands grew cold. And Jardine's baby boy was still dead.

This time, Cap let the tears fall. His shoulders shook as he fought against the emotions that tore at his insides, and lost. He'd failed. His mysterious power had left him, if he'd ever had it in the first place. Father, the man he'd long looked up to and admired, had allowed Lum to treat Cap with cruelty. Just as bad, he'd stood silent while Lum stole the tiny body of a friend's child. And Cap knew that he himself was hardly any better. He'd joined the grave robbers and kept silent, even after he realized how much pain he was inflicting on others. All for money.

For Mamma, Cap told himself, angrily wiping his dripping nose on his coat sleeve. *But I didn't understand until now that it wasn't worth it.*

At that moment, footsteps pounded in the hall outside the room. The door that connected Cap's tiny workshop with the main house flew open and banged against the wall with a loud clatter. Hands seized him by the arm.

"Gimme that," Lum hissed, snatching the bundle from the table. His twisted face was more sinister than ever in the lantern light. "You worthless half-wit! Too bad Noah didn't throw you off the boat when you were born! Coulda saved us all a heap of trouble." With that, he shoved Cap so hard the boy fell to his knees.

Struggling to his feet, Cap noticed Father there, with his hands in his pockets and his head down. "Father?" he said, but his voice died away. What was there to say to this man, this sudden stranger?

"Go to bed, Cap," Father said in a soft voice. He turned and followed Lum out of the room. Their footsteps died away. The front door thudded.

Go to bed? Cap laughed once, a short, mirthless sound that echoed in the tiny room. Then he reached out and extinguished the quivering flame of his lantern. Pocketing some matches and a candle stub, he exited his workshop through the narrow outer door and crouched for a moment beneath his willow tree.

"I'll go to bed, all right," he whispered. "After I take care of one more job." Gritting his teeth, he followed the men, though he knew exactly where they were going. Once they arrived at the Round House, Cap hung in the shadows and watched until they handed over their quarry and slunk off. Then, he snuck around the building.

Someone had finally thought to close the basement window that led to the dissection room, but no one had thought to latch it. Cap climbed inside, lit his candle, and began his search.

One room was full of broken crates. Another contained a row of empty pickle barrels. The chamber reeked of whiskey. A locked door, marked "supplies," wouldn't budge despite Cap's rough shaking and a final kick at the unyielding wood. The baby had to be here, somewhere.

Out of ideas, Cap left the basement. When he reached the main floor, he nearly dropped his candle at the sound of voices that drew closer. Recovering his wits barely in time, he cupped his hand over the fluttering flame and backed down a few steps. There was the soft, wordless murmur of a man's deep tones. Then, in response, another voice whined: "It is *not* my fault!"

Those words echoed through the circular front hall of the building. It was unmistakable: Dr. Rusch was here! But who was the other man? Could it be Lum? The footsteps passed the stairwell, then moved upward. Holding his hand over the flame, Cap crept after them while a thick hatred welled up inside.

The voices moved to the second floor and disappeared. Creeping inch by inch, Cap finally reached the top of the stairs. A weak light shone from under one of the doors. Putting his ear to the keyhole, he could make out a few words here and there. Dr. Rusch continued to wail in a shrill voice:

"No one suspects anything! And why should I not take a few souvenirs, here and there?"

A soft, muffled response.

"Columbus Jones? That buffoon? He's happy as long as he gets his payment. Never asks any questions."

More muffled sounds.

"That was an accident, man! I could have sworn he was dead! Same as the other man, and the girl! I cannot explain it!"

A jolt passed through Cap.

"I've always followed your orders!" Dr. Rusch growled.

The words burned themselves itself into Cap's brain. He gasped aloud. If Dr. Rusch followed orders, he was not the man in charge of this resurrection business. So, who was?

"Wait!"

The voice was now loud in the boy's ear. The doorknob rattled. Cap extinguished his candle, leapt away, and hid himself on the other side of a massive cabinet.

The door slammed and rapid footsteps pounded away. Cap sank down to the floor, willing himself to breathe silently. Moments later, the door opened again and a second set of footsteps stumbled at an uneven pace across the landing and began to descend the stairs.

"No, wait! I wanted that specimen!" Dr. Rusch said.

Cap was torn. Blast it all, he wanted to follow and discover who that mysterious man was. But Jardine's baby was still missing, and what Dr. Rusch had just said made Cap certain the tiny body was nearby. When the silence was complete, he moved back to the door where he'd heard the voices. It was unlocked.

Cap crept inside the room and eased the door closed behind him. *God, for once, bless me with a little luck*, he prayed. *I sure could use it about now.*

TWENTY-SEVEN

ONCE INSIDE, HE turned on the gas lamps and spied a metal plaque on the wall: *Dr. Abraham Rusch*. Books and papers were scattered everywhere. The air was stale and smelled of tobacco, spirits, and unwashed bodies. But what caught Cap's attention the most were the shelves on the opposite wall. They were filled with boxes of all sizes. The room looked more like a dry goods store than the examining room of a medical doctor.

A tall mirror stood in the corner, and on a dress form beside it was a man's formal coat with tails. On a side table, gold watches, earrings, cuff links, and necklaces gleamed on a blue velvet cloth, like a display in a jeweler's shop. Cap's heart sprang into action— maybe Jessamyn's ruby ring was here.

He sorted through the pile of jewelry. There were many rings, including several with diamonds in them, but no red stones. Cap's shoulders slumped. He stood back and blew out his breath in a long stream.

A cuckoo clock wheezed and chimed from its perch on the wall. Cap nearly jumped out of his own skin as the tiny wooden bird hooted the time.

"Blast," he muttered. It was after midnight. Mamma must be frantic.

She's been abed all evening. She likely doesn't even know I'm gone, he reassured himself. But what about Father? Could *he* be worried?

Cap closed his eyes at the painful reminder of the man who had allowed Columbus Jones to treat him so harshly. Father repeatedly allowed Lum to heap ugly words and abuse upon his own son.

Father doesn't care. He likely hopes I won't come back.

Trying to ignore the aching inside his chest, the boy threw another glance at the cuckoo clock and stopped short with a furrowed brow. As the chimes concluded and the tiny bird ducked back inside its little door, painted figures began to dance, and a waterwheel turned.

"What in the blazes?" he blurted. Cap gaped at the wall. That was Mr. Garrett's clock! He'd never seen another like it anywhere.

A sick feeling settled into Cap's protesting stomach. Old Dr. Rusch was stealing from the dead. Nothing else explained all the things he'd piled away in this room. It was practically like a pirate's cave full of treasure!

So, what did that mean about Mr. Garrett?

"Nothing," Cap told himself. "Mr. Garrett's fine." Squaring his shoulders, he picked up his candle again. He couldn't worry now about his old friend. First things first: he still needed to find Jardine's baby, and if it wasn't in this room, it surely would be in another one.

He made a face at the lingering smell in Dr. Rusch's office while he extinguished the gas lamps. In a flash, words Lum had once spoken to him came back:

"I'll pack you in whiskey and send you off to a place no one'll ever find you."

Whiskey? It could be no coincidence that a room downstairs reeked of the stuff. A quick search of the doctor's desk revealed a set of keys, which Cap pocketed. Holding his breath, he pushed the door open with a shaky hand, but the round building was silent. The boy hurried back to the basement.

After trying a few keys, the door marked "supplies" opened with a screech. He stepped inside and held his candle aloft. Many barrels were crowded into the room. The smell of whiskey made his eyes water and burn.

Coughing, he searched through a cupboard until he found what he was looking for; a metal file that looked solid enough to pry up a sealed lid. He placed his candle stub upon a windowsill and began. The first lid came off easily. As the smell of whiskey filled the air, Cap gaped in horror at the sight below him. Just below the surface of the liquid was a head of curly hair.

Replacing the lid, Cap gagged and fought to keep his supper from making a return appearance. He could hardly believe his eyes. If all these barrels were full, the number of bodies inside them was much greater than the number of poor stiffs he had helped dig up.

Swiping his arm over his face to wipe away the stinging tears caused by the fumes in the room, Cap moved to the next barrel, and the next.

Bodies of assorted sizes were jammed inside, all soaked in the alcoholic mixture. All adults. Six, seven, eight. Cap worked feverishly, the whiskey stench making his head swim. No baby. Eleven, twelve, thirteen. Still no luck.

Cap's shoulders drooped. The baby had to be here! One barrel stood against the wall, uncovered. The boy hardly spared it a glance. Then, he shrugged and hurried over to check it for good measure. He held his candle stub aloft to peer inside.

Dr. Rusch stared back. His sightless, bloodshot eyes were wide in his upturned head.

"Holy Mary!" Cap shrieked. He dropped his candle. The room plunged into darkness.

While his heart tried to beat itself out of his chest, Cap scrabbled around on the floor until he found his candle. With shaking hand, he had to strike a match several times before he managed to relight the wick.

Despite the bile that rose to the back of his throat, Cap couldn't help inching closer to the barrel and its grisly contents. The dead man wore rings on every finger. There, winking in the flickering glow of the tiny candle, was a ring set with a red stone on the man's little finger.

Placing his candle onto the lid of a neighboring barrel, Cap whispered a quick prayer, just in case someone decided to listen in and help him for once.

"Bless me with courage and nimble fingers," he muttered. "And a way to escape this infernal place. Amen."

Rolling up his sleeves, Cap seized Dr. Rusch's hand. The ring was stuck. The boy pulled as hard as he could, but it wouldn't budge. His eyes stung from the fumes. The solution in the barrel sloshed as Cap struggled to wrest the ring from the doctor's finger.

"Move, blast you!" Cap hissed, sweating and swearing at all the saints. The ring finally moved, ever so slightly. He pulled harder. Suddenly it was clenched tight in his fist.

Blessed be our Lady of Mercy, Cap prayed, though he was fairly certain God's mother would sternly disapprove of his recent actions.

"Lots of nice, sharp knives in the next room. Want me to fetch one for you?" a gravelly voice said from behind. "You can cut that finger clean off." The man chuckled.

Shrieking, Cap whirled and dropped his candle once more. This time, the room remained well-lit from the glow of a lantern held aloft by a grizzled man. It was Parsons, the "hero" who'd offered to guard the cemetery. The light gave the man's wizened face a sinister yellow cast.

"You can't stay away, can you, boy?" Parsons said, shuffling into the room with a jagged smile on his face. "A little thief, are you? Know what we do to thieves?"

"It's you," Cap blurted, while a dawning horror punched him in the gut. "You're the one who killed him!"

Parsons's bushy white eyebrows met in the middle. "Killed who, boy? I ain't done nothin' to nobody!" He shuffled forward, and Cap backed up until he slammed into the cold stone wall.

"Now you leave be this poor old croaker," Parsons said, setting the lantern onto the floor nearby. He began to shove Dr. Rusch farther inside the barrel. "What'd he ever do to—" Then the man stopped and his toothless mouth gaped wide as he blinked down at the body. "Land o' Goshen!" he shouted. "It's Dr. Rusch! What have you done to him?"

TWENTY-EIGHT

C AP BOLTED. H E hurtled through the dark doorway and up
the stairs, clutching the ring in his fist.

"Murderer!" Parsons screamed. "Murderer!"

There's only one person who can help me, Cap thought as he fled.
Please, God, let him be here! Dr. Ivins's new office was on the third
floor, and Jardine said he usually slept there.

A light shone under the doctor's door. Cap's shoulders
slumped in relief. *Not all the saints and angels have abandoned me*,
he thought. He knocked. There was only silence in response, so
Cap pounded.

As the door swung open, the boy blinked as the light from
glowing gas lamps hit his eyes.

"Cap Cooper?" Dr. Ivins said. The man's crumpled jacket hung open, and his shirt was crinkled and dirty. Something about the doctor's hair was strange, but Cap had other matters to think of and dismissed all else from his mind.

"Please, sir, I didn't kill him!" he blurted. "Parsons thinks I did, but it wasn't me! Honest!"

Dr. Ivins gaped at him.

As Cap stared back, he suddenly realized what was strange about the man's hair. It was skewed. Dr. Ivins looked as if he wore a brown coonskin cap, stuck sideways onto his bald head. Dr. Ivins noticed Cap's gaze and quickly reached up to straighten his wig.

"Come in," Dr. Ivins said in a short voice. He grabbed Cap's arm and pulled him inside, closing the door behind the boy. "What are you saying, son?"

"I ... I found him," Cap said, gulping. "Dr. Rusch. He's down in the basement in the room with all the barrels, but I didn't kill him, I swear it!"

Dr. Ivins's eyebrows shot up to his wig. "*What?*"

In a shaky voice, Cap did his best to describe what he'd seen and heard. He paused for breath, and silence fell. The boy's arm began to throb where Dr. Ivins's long fingers dug into his skin. The man's face was incredulous. Cap's heart turned to lead.

He doesn't believe me, he thought.

"You heard him speak to someone? Did you know the other man's voice?" Dr. Ivins finally asked.

"No, sir. The voice was too quiet," Cap answered.

Dr. Ivins's face visibly relaxed. He released Cap's arm and moved around to the other side of his desk, where he fished about until he pulled out a pipe. "It seems we have a rather odd situation," the man said, with a half-smile. "Allow me to indulge myself for a moment, son. I like to have a smoke while I think."

"Aren't you going to call the sheriff, sir?" Cap asked. He rubbed his arm where the doctor had grabbed him. Dr. Ivins lit his pipe and blew smoke rings toward the cracked ceiling.

"I imagine Parsons will already have taken care of that. He's very efficient," he said.

What little remaining courage Cap had plummeted to his boots. He swallowed. "But do you believe me, sir?" he asked.

"Oh, I believe you, son, I believe you," Dr. Ivins said with a slight smile that was no more than a twitch at the corners of his mouth. He took a long draw from his pipe and blew out the smoke in a stream. The bittersweet scent of the smoke filled the room.

"What I'd like to know now is why you came here in the first place." He cocked his head to the side and gazed at the boy.

"I, well," Cap said, and stopped, confused. Why wasn't Dr. Ivins more upset when he learned that another doctor had been found dead down below? Surely, he was, but he must want to make certain that Cap was being truthful. The boy had many secrets to hide, but their weight had become far too heavy to bear. He'd already decided to tell someone, and it was high time. He could trust Dr. Ivins. He had to. Cap made his decision and took a deep breath.

"I was looking for a body," he said, with a sudden rush of relief to have the truth come out. "I'm a snatcher, sir. I work with the men who dig up bodies for the college." Cap held up his hands as

Dr. Ivins blinked at him. "Please, hear me out! I've been having my doubts, you see. I don't want to do it anymore. It isn't right. Anyway, another snatcher took a baby right after the funeral, and that didn't set none too well with me. The baby belongs to a friend of mine, and I wanted to get it back for her."

Dr. Ivins slowly put his pipe down onto his desk. A tic had developed near his right eye. The blood drained from the man's face, turning his skin a pasty gray color. The man stood.

"Sir?" Cap asked. He took another a step back. "You're not going to have me arrested, are you?"

"*You* are a snatcher?" Dr. Ivins asked in a hoarse voice.

"Yes, sir," Cap answered.

"Who do you work for?" Dr. Ivins asked, moving closer so that his face was inches from the boy's. His voice was a mere whisper and his eyes never left Cap's face. "Tell me."

"Columbus Jones. And *he* was working for Dr. Rusch. At least I thought so. But now, after hearing Rusch talk to someone else, well, I don't know."

"I see," Ivins murmured. Something in his eyes made Cap shrink away from the man.

At that moment, tiny orange flames crackled to life on top of the paper-strewn desk. "Fire!" Cap shouted, pointing. Dr. Ivins whirled, his wig flying askew once more, and darted to his desk.

"Damnable pipe," he said, whipping off his jacket to smother the flames.

Without really thinking about why he wanted to run, Cap moved toward the door. As he did so, he bumped into a trunk that sat upon the floor. He glanced down and froze.

"Sakes alive," he breathed out. Inside the trunk were several glass containers. Each held a tiny body floating in clear liquid. Beside them was a burlap-wrapped bundle, shaped like a doll.

Cap dove, seized the bundle and bolted.

Dr. Ivins's shouts echoed after him. "Help, Parsons! He's here! The boy is here! Call the sheriff! Paarsooons!!"

TWENTY-NINE

C AP SPRINTED TO the front doors and yanked on the knobs.
They wouldn't budge. "No!" he shouted, kicking at the im-
prisoning wood. A loud rapping at the nearby window made him
yelp. He whirled to see a figure peering in at him, hands cupped
against the glass to see inside. A muffled voice shouted his name.

The boy's heart flopped about inside his chest like a fish on a
riverbank. "Jessamyn?" he called. What in the world? He darted
to the window and lifted the sill. Blessedly, it heaved open with a
groan. Cap dove headfirst outside and landed in a heap at Jessamyn's feet, still clutching the tiny bundle to his chest.

"What's happening—"

"What are you—"

The two spoke at the same time. Jessamyn was clad in her blue dress, but had only a thin shawl about her shoulders. The girl was shivering in the cold.

"We'll talk later. Run!" Cap shouted, seizing her hand.

The two fled, leaving the college behind them and hurtling downtown, past shops opening for the day. No one came after them, though a milkman squinted in their direction and shook his head as he left clanking bottles upon a doorstep.

Finally, they slowed down to cross a street. Cap kept glancing behind them, but it seemed no one had pursued them. At least, not yet.

"Why were you outside the college?" Cap asked, his breath coming in quick gasps. "The sun's hardly up."

Jessamyn's features twisted into a look of such distress, Cap thought she'd cry.

"I spied on that Mr. Jones," she said. Her eyes were enormous. "I heard him talking about the bodies stolen from the cemetery. He said they needed to lay low for a while, or they'd be caught for sure. And then Sister Mariah said—" The girl's voice broke, and she took a deep breath. "She said she hoped it wouldn't be for long, because she needed more money. Oh, Cap, she's working with that awful man, somehow!"

That's why Sister Mariah acted so all-fired suspicious. She knows I was working with Lum, Cap thought. He hung his head.

"Jessamyn, I'm real..." the boy began to say, but he stopped and cleared his throat. Jessamyn didn't seem to know *he* was in on it, too, and for now he had to keep it that way. He vowed he'd come clean, but now wasn't the time.

"So, you ran away?" he said instead.

The girl nodded. "You see, I've been sick again. Sister Mariah promised me I'd get well, but I always felt worse every time I took the medicine the doctor left for me. So last night, I pretended to take it but spilled it onto my blankets when she wasn't looking. When I woke up, I felt better than I had for days. I went down to the kitchen to get something to eat, but Sister Mariah was there, drinking tea with Mr. Jones. That's when I heard what they said."

"That must have been a shock," Cap finally managed to say.

The girl nodded. "But that's not the only reason I ran," she said. Tears made glittering trails down her cheeks. "The sexton was there, carrying out little Caroline, another orphan like me. She was dead. She's only six. They said she got sick like I did."

"Golly," Cap whispered. He tried to swallow, but couldn't.

"I grabbed Sister Mariah's shawl and followed the sexton to the college. Oh, I don't know what I was going to do, but I wanted to look inside. That's when I saw you and heard all that yelling. Why were *you* there, Cap?" the girl asked.

"I was looking for Dr. Ivins. His new office is there." Cap hurried on, hoping the girl wouldn't wonder how he got inside a building that was locked. "And I don't know exactly what's going on, but it's something real awful. Dr. Rusch got himself killed!"

Jessamyn's mouth gaped open.

"We best keep moving," Cap said. They ran on, while Cap struggled to think. Where *could* they go? Then, he thought of the bundle he still held in his arms. Swiftly, he removed his coat and wrapped it around the body, glancing at Jessamyn to see if she noticed.

"Come on," he said. "I'll tell you more in a minute." Cap led the girl through a litter-strewn back garden. They squeezed through a gap in a splintered fence and emerged onto a narrow dirt track that ran behind crowded houses.

"Where are we?" Jessamyn asked.

"I have a friend nearby. We can ask her for help. I, uh, I have to bring her something."

Jessamyn backed up a few steps. "No," she said, shaking her head. "I have to go back to St. Joseph's."

"What?" Cap said, squinting at the girl. "You heard Sister Mariah! If she's in on that resurrection scheme, well, she's the last person you want to see!"

"She doesn't know I heard her talk. Anyway, there's somebody I need to get out of there."

"Who?"

Flushing, the girl looked away. "A friend."

Turning her back, Jessamyn started to walk away with her shoulders hunched against the cold. Her head was down and her steps rapid. It called to mind the time she'd left school, after leaving that note for Cap. His insides twisted. He had to stop her. He plunged his hand into his pocket and seized the ring he'd wrested from Dr. Rusch's finger.

"Wait!" he called. "Is this yours?" He held it out.

The girl turned around. Spying the tiny gold circlet in Cap's palm, her eyes widened.

"Yes," she breathed. "Cap, however did you find it?" She flew to him, seized the ring, and slid it onto her finger.

"Dr. Rusch had it," Cap said. "He has a whole room full of things he's filched from the dead. Lum was working for him, so my guess is he took it when he thought you were a goner."

Jessamyn held her hand out to admire the stone. It sparkled in the early morning sun. A tear slid down her cheek.

"I'm so glad to have it back," she whispered. "It's only thing my father left for me."

Cap took a deep breath. "Your mother will be happy, too, I reckon," he said softly.

"Oh, yes—" Jessamyn stopped and her face nearly turned the color of the crimson-painted fence nearby. "I mean, I…"

"It's all right. I know about your mamma," Cap told her.

"Why, I reckon you do," Jessamyn said with bitterness. "All those awful boys at school tease me so. I don't know how they found out, but…"

The girl grew silent as a brown-skinned woman with several chins popped through the door of a neighboring house and eyed them with open curiosity, her shrewd eyes pinning them as she threw out a pan of dishwater.

"Look, Cap, I should go home, now," Jessamyn said. "Thank you for finding my ring. I'll never forget it." She bit her lip. "But you and I, we just can't be friends."

"Why?" Cap breathed. But Jessamyn turned away. The listening woman was still outside her door with the empty dishpan in her hands, wearing a look of frank curiosity on her face.

Cap hurried after the girl. "Wait," he blurted. "I know about your mother, because I've met her."

Jessamyn whirled. "When? How?" The staring woman moved several steps closer with her head cocked to one side. She placed her dishpan on the ground and dried her hands on her red calico apron.

"That day I went to St. Joseph's looking for you, I ended up in her room by mistake," Cap said while his face stung. "She talked to me. She was nice."

"Nice," Jessamyn said with a mirthless laugh. "I know you hear what those boys say. You don't really think that."

Cap's face grew even hotter. "But I do," he said.

Jessamyn turned away. "It's not only what my mamma does," she whispered. "It's my father." The girl pulled her long braid over her shoulder and stared at the ground. "Folks know he and Mamma ran off together. They know he was a slave." Jessamyn turned back to Cap and waited, her eyes searching his face.

"A slave?" Cap repeated, swallowing hard. "But that means that he, uh, that you…"

"I'm a half-breed," Jessamyn said. Her eyes were round. "A girl who doesn't belong anywhere." She gazed at Cap with an expression so lost it made his insides smart something awful. "I'm the daughter of a former slave and a fallen woman. That's why Mamma thought I'd be better off if everyone thought I was an orphan."

Cap scuffed the ground with the toe of his boot. "I never guessed," he finally said. "I mean, you look, well…" he gave up and picked a bit of dirt from under his ragged nails.

"I look white," Jessamyn said softly. "Mamma irons my hair. We came here after my father died, looking for his family, but we never found them. Mamma decided it was best if I passed for white when she looked for work, trying to keep us fed. But she never found enough to support us until…oh, never mind." The girl turned her back to Cap, but not before he saw the gleam of tears in her eyes.

"It doesn't matter," Cap said. "It does not matter one bit."

Jessamyn bowed her head. "I wish that were true," she said in a voice rough with tears.

Cap took a deep breath. "I heard your mamma talking to someone," he said. "She said she had no other way to take care of you. I can't help thinking she's not all that bad. I mean, if she was so all-fired wicked, I guess she'd have just left you."

"The boy's right, child," the staring woman said. Cap and Jessamyn both whipped their heads around.

"No good woman would ever leave her own baby if she could help it," she added, swinging her dishpan as she turned to walk back to her house. "And I opine it's no bad woman who's only doing what she's gotta do to feed her little one."

She smiled wide while Cap and Jessamyn stared. "It's no bad woman who chose to love like she did—loving somebody nobody else thought was worth a lick. That's what I think. What was his name, by the way?" she asked. "You mind me asking your daddy's name?"

Jessamyn didn't speak. The woman shrugged and smiled at them. "God bless you, child," she said. She retreated inside her house and the door closed behind her with a squeak.

"She's right," Cap said. "Your mamma isn't so wicked as people say, and you're the nicest girl I ever met. I mean that."

"Oh, Cap," Jessamyn said, in a voice still thick with tears.

A window squealed open somewhere nearby, and Cap clenched his fists. Land sakes, but they were becoming a spectacle! Who was watching them now? He held his coat-wrapped bundle more tightly to his chest.

"Come with me," he begged. "Please! We need to ask for help."

To his relief, Jessamyn nodded and followed. Cap led her around a side yard and onto a sagging front porch.

Please, God, let this work, Cap prayed. *If it doesn't, I'm plumb out of ideas, unless that nosy lady with all the chins will take us in.*

THIRTY

"HELLO, THERE," DELPHIA said. "It's a bit early to call, isn't it?"

"This is my friend Jessamyn," Cap blurted. "Please, we need help. May we come in?"

Delphia waved them inside. The warm kitchen smelled of corn cakes and maple syrup. The older girl told them to sit and fried more cakes at the stove while throwing curious glances over her shoulder.

Cap remained standing. The bundle in his arms seemed to grow heavy for a moment. A suffocating guilt surged through him. He needed to right a wrong.

"Now, you sit, Cap Cooper. Might as well put some food in your belly. Then you can tell me what it is I can do for you," Delphia said, placing a platter of cakes on the table.

"Is your mother here?" Cap asked, hardly able to breathe. "Or your father?"

"No. Mamma's out tending a patient. Father told her she should stay home and rest, but you know Mamma." Delphia said with a tiny smile. "And Father left at dawn to wait outside the mayor's office. He wants to talk to him about that awful business at the cemetery," she said, while a frown replaced her smile. "He doesn't think Mr. Parsons is the right fellow for the guarding job."

Cap glanced down at the bundle in his arms.

I could give it to Delphia…no! he thought. *She might not understand. I must give the baby to his mother.* Swallowing hard, Cap placed his wadded coat with its fragile contents beneath his chair, while guilt roiled inside him. Delphia put a hot corn cake on his plate, and the sight of the food made his stomach churn. He mumbled a quick "no, thank you." Cap watched the two others eat, unable to keep still. He jiggled one knee in a nervous rhythm until Delphia shot him such a severe look he grabbed both legs to keep them still.

When the girls had finished, Delphia stood to clear away the plates. Jessamyn rose to help her.

"Thank you," Delphia told her. "It's Jessamyn, right?" The girl nodded.

"She's why we came here," Cap said. "She needs a place to stay until we know she'll be safe."

Delphia's eyes widened. "Safe? From what?" she asked.

"From the resurrectionists," Cap said in a low voice. "Sister Mariah is one of them."

This time, Delphia's eyebrows rose right up to her hairline, almost disappearing under the bright red ribbon she'd used to tie back her black curls. "I think you'd best explain, Cap Cooper.

That can't be true," she said, placing the plates back down onto the table with a clatter.

"Sister Mariah was talking about it with Mr. Jones, the man who does repairs at the orphanage," Jessamyn said in a tiny voice. "I heard it with my own ears."

"Lord have mercy," Delphia said, gasping for air. She held her hand to her heart. "Are you telling me the truth?" she demanded.

"It's true," Cap told her. "Your mother warned me about Mr. Jones. She said she and your father were real suspicious of him." He glanced down while a guilty flush made his face sting.

Delphia gazed from one to the other, an incredulous look on her face. Then, her eyes narrowed.

"I knew he had to be involved," she said. "That awful, mean, *wicked* old man." She paused to take a deep breath. "I can see how Mr. Jones would tangle himself up in something so unjust, but Sister Mariah?" Delphia raised her eyes to the ceiling and shook her head. "That I do not understand."

"Listen," Cap said. "I must go, but Jessamyn needs to stay here. Please, tell me where your mother went. After I talk to her, I'll come back and explain everything. I promise."

Even though you'll likely never want to speak to me again, he thought.

Delphia began to pace the kitchen with a crinkled brow. She took several turns about the tiny room and then stopped short and squared her shoulders.

"Cap, you and I must go to Dr. Ivins at once," she said. "And then to the sheriff. They'll know what to do."

"No—" Cap blurted. Everyone jumped at the sound of a fist pounding on the door.

"Please," Cap said, bolting to his feet. "Don't let anyone know we're here. I'll explain after whoever this is leaves."

For a few, painful heartbeats, Delphia hesitated. Then, she pressed her lips together. "All right, Cap," she whispered. "I'll see who's at the door. Go on upstairs and hide in my bedroom. First one on the right." She rushed from the kitchen, closing the door behind her.

Cap and Jessamyn fled to a small, sparsely furnished bedroom. Books covered every surface. A diagram of the nervous system was tacked up on one wall, a finely detailed drawing of a skeleton on another. The boy crept to the window that faced the street and peered out. An old black carriage stood out front.

Dr. Ivins! Cap gripped the windowsill until his knuckles turned white. *No!*

"Wait here," he whispered to Jessamyn. Her dark eyes were wide in her pale face. She nodded. The boy crept to the head of the stairs.

Muffled voices came from the front room. Cap strained to listen, but could not decipher their words. Dr. Ivins's voice, a deep baritone, rose and fell in a ragged rhythm. The man spoke faster and faster.

The voices moved closer, so Cap bolted back into Delphia's room. Jessamyn's face was ashen. They waited, hardly daring to breathe. A minute passed, then two, then three. A cold sweat crept all over Cap's body.

Finally, unmistakable sounds told them the carriage was pulling away. He and Jessamyn waited several minutes for Delphia, but she didn't come. Children shouted as they headed to school and horses clip-clopped on the street outside. A man called out that he had tin ware to sell. Delphia still didn't come.

Finally, Cap could stand it no longer. He crept down to the kitchen, holding his breath. Delphia was alone, sitting at the table with her back to him.

"Delphia?" Cap asked. "I must talk to you about Dr. Ivins."

Delphia stood and turned around. She held something in her arms. Her face was streaked with tears.

"No," Cap breathed out. His limbs grew heavy. He'd forgotten the bundle! His empty coat lay upon the floor, and Delphia held her tiny brother's body in her arms.

"I didn't believe him," Delphia said in a ragged voice. "He said *you* were helping that gang of ghouls steal bodies for the college. The bodies of my neighbors. My friends." Her eyes were filled with disbelief. "He even told me he saw you early this morning, leaving a room where they found Dr. Rusch dead."

Cap shook his head wildly and tried to speak, but couldn't.

Delphia's words came out in harsh sobs. "I never told him you were here. I told him you were a good boy, Cap. I swore you were! Then I came back in here and found your coat on the floor, so I picked it up."

She stood tall, cradling the tiny body in her arms, and glared into Cap's face, her own shining with tears. "This is *my family*. I will never forgive you, Captain Cooper. From now on until forever. I promise you that," she said between clenched teeth.

"Please, Delphia, let me explain," Cap said. "It's not what you think."

"You go on out of here," Delphia yelled. "The girl can stay, so she'll be safe from you. You leave. Now." Cap saw the steel in her eyes. He knew she wouldn't listen. Not now, perhaps not ever.

"What is it?" Jessamyn asked, hurrying into the kitchen. "Cap, what's going on?"

"NOW!" Delphia screamed.

"I'm sorry," Cap said, snatching his coat from the floor. Jessamyn stared at the tiny baby in Delphia's arms with a look of horror. The older girl's face was a mask of wounded fury.

Cap fled.

THIRTY-ONE

CAP STUMBLED AS he walked along, trying to stick close to doorways as he kept a lookout for Dr. Ivins. People were a dark blur, the sky a bright smear to his swollen eyes. His shoulders sagged. He was cold, deathly afraid, and had no idea where to go. If he went home, Ivins would surely find him.

A flash of blue caught his eye. Across the street, a woman was climbing steep stairs that clung to the side of a sagging house. Her face was mostly covered by a black veil, but a tawny curl hung from under her hat. Cap's heart leapt. It was Tillie!

He followed. Tillie would be bound to help him, wouldn't she, after he told her Jessamyn was safe? He waited until the woman had gone inside and counted to ten before creeping up the stairs. He tried the knob. It was unlocked. Cap let out the air he'd been holding unconsciously in a long sigh. The door opened onto a dark hallway and muffled voices came from somewhere ahead. A rat pattered across the wood floor, its tiny claws scratching.

The boy crept forward, straining to see in the dark. He passed an open doorway and nearly gasped out loud at the sight of the room's contents. Round barrels were stacked floor to ceiling. Cap darted inside the room so he could read the labels pasted onto the barrels in the dim light filtering through the grimy windows.

Abraham's Cucumber Pickles. Crisp and Delicious. Leaning closer, Cap caught a strong whiff of whiskey and wrinkled his nose.

Ivins and Rusch must have been shipping all those extra bodies to other schools, he thought with a start. There were so many! Were these all the people who died from the strange illness? Had they all had that "arrangement," so nobody had to bother digging them up?

He returned to the dark hallway and his search for Tillie. He came to a door covered with a faded green fabric. The door was cracked open and voices floated out. Cap inched closer, straining to listen.

"Where is my daughter?" Tillie begged in a raw voice. "You were the last to see her. You must know something!"

"I have no idea where she is." Cap held his breath while his insides turned to ice as he recognized Dr. Ivins's voice. "She must be with that Cooper boy, the one we're looking for. They were seen approaching the train station, but they can't have gone far, Tillie. I assure you we'll find her."

Slowly shaking his head, the boy sucked in his breath. Dr. Ivins was telling folks that he, Cap, *kidnapped* Jessamyn!

A familiar, throaty voice spoke, and Cap stiffened. "Surely he wouldn't leave town with Jessamyn so ill. I don't understand why he would take her, doctor. I know he was sweet on her, but I can't believe he'd put the girl in harm's way."

Cap's mind whirled. So he'd find no help from Tillie. Then, he froze at the sound of Sister Mariah's voice. Her words chilled Cap to the marrow of his bones.

"Well, now we must find poor Jessamyn *and* find a way to keep the boy from talking! This business isn't for children! You should never have let Cooper bring his son—"

"I had no idea the boy was involved," Dr. Ivins snapped. "I blame that fool brother of yours. He must have had a hand in it."

Licking dry lips, Cap inched backward. What exactly did she plan to do to keep him from talking? He tried to creep away, on slow, steady feet. That was his mistake. His boots squeaked on the floor.

The green door banged open, and Dr. Ivins plunged into the hallway. As his eyes met Cap's, he smiled.

Whirling to run, Cap tripped and fell. Yellow stabs of light exploded in his eyes as he struck his head. Rough hands seized him. Cap felt his body rise through the air, and then sink down, down into a soft, inky blackness.

H E WAS COLD. The cold filled his body and seeped into his bones. They weren't bones at all, but ice. He was a boy made of winter, a skeleton of icicles surrounded by flesh of snow.

Cap tried to speak, but his tongue was sluggish. He opened his eyes, but saw nothing. Thick darkness surrounded him. It was over him, beneath him, and all around him.

Moaning, Cap turned his head from side to side. With the movement came the pain, dull at first, then growing in intensity, pounding, searing, bringing tears to his eyes. He cried out as a tender lump on one side of his head scraped against a hard surface.

Where am I?

More feeling came back, along with more pain. He wiggled his toes and tried to stretch out. Then, he felt the ropes, wound tight and knotted around his thin frame.

The air was stale and damp, smelling of earth and decay. It brought to mind the time, not so long ago, when Cap had dug into his first grave. Nellie's grave. Moaning from the pain, Cap tried to sit up. The ropes were too tight. He could barely lift his head. He tried instead to raise his feet. His scuffed boots met with something solid, inches above his body. The dull *thud* echoed in Cap's ears.

No. It can't be!

He moved his feet sideways. The result was the same: a solid surface only inches to his right. Moving to the left produced the same results.

He was inside a coffin. And if the surrounding silence told him anything, that coffin was buried, deep.

"Cap Cooper," he whispered, "you're in a fine mess now."

He had no idea how much time passed. No birds sang. No wind sighed as it moved the tree branches. No solid kitchen clock ticked away the seconds, the minutes, the hours. The only sounds were the hissing of Cap's breath and the beating of his heart.

It was the silence that got to him.

He sang every song Mamma used to sing to him as a baby, the hymns Mrs. Hardy had taught him, and the rough sailor's tunes Father sang when he thought no one was listening. His thick tongue barely worked, and the words came out wrong, but it helped to hear his voice.

He prayed. At first, he had no words. There was only a longing that filled his heart, so strong he was sure that someone, somewhere, had to feel it. Then, he spoke the names of all the saints Mrs. Hardy had ever taught him. Mary and Joseph. St. John the Baptist. St. Andrew. St. Barbara the Healer. Ethelfleda. Cap couldn't remember what she did, but Mrs. Hardy had mentioned her once.

Strangely, no fear quickened the blood in his veins. The only thought that filled his head was the desire to see again. To move out of this thick blackness, to have it peeled away until there was a glimmer of light. To hear again; the sounds of the horses' hooves as they clopped along the cobbled streets, the shouts as other boys ran and scuffled in the schoolyard. Father's laugh. The soft sigh of his mother's voice.

You understand, God. Don't you? It was all for Mamma. We needed the money.

Cap closed his eyes. *We were wrong.*

He slept but awoke once, coughing. The air was stale. It felt thick, like a chilled soup he struggled to drag into his lungs, while he tried not to think about how long it would be until he could no longer breathe.

He went back to sleep. He dreamt he was in the classroom, called to the board to solve an impossible equation. Tangled numbers covered the board and were even scrawled across the whitewashed walls.

Master Rankin walked to the head of the classroom and began to scrape his fingernails down the length of the blackboard. The screeching noise hurt Cap's ears. He'd go mad from the sound! He tried to raise his hands to cover his ears, but his arms were stuck to his sides.

Cap opened his eyes. The darkness was no longer so thick. The air was cold. More metallic screeches filled his ears. A muffled voice muttered and laughed. Then, the blackness above his head lifted away. Blinking, Cap saw tiny pinpoints of light, shimmering high above him, and a dark form that towered over him.

"Well, lookie here," Lum said, crouching down inside the grave until his face was inches from Cap's own. "This thing ain't gone bad yet."

Cap tried to speak but was seized by rough hands and yanked from his broken coffin. Then, the man jammed a wad of cloth into his mouth and covered Cap's head with a moldering potato sack.

"Time for a ride, boy," Lum said. "If it was left to me, I'd a just left you there to rot, but the Doc changed his mind. Has other plans for you."

Lum lifted Cap as though he were no more than a half-filled sack of potatoes and tossed him into the back of a wagon. The boy's head pounded again as it impacted against the solid wood. The vehicle lurched into movement.

Before long, the wagon stopped. Cap was lifted again and slung over Lum's broad shoulder. Then, a single sharp knock, followed by three more knocks rang out in the cold air. It was then that Cap understood where he'd been taken.

Oh, no.

THIRTY-TWO

Dizzy and sickened, Cap was tossed down like a sack of refuse. The back of his head thudded hard onto a table.

"Here's the good doctor's next...*dissection*," Lum said.

Cap forced the cloth from his mouth and tried to speak. He croaked.

"You hear something?" Lum asked.

"I ain't heard nothing," someone said with a chuckle. Parsons.

"Fancy a pint at Mooney's?"

"Thank you kindly."

Lum dropped his massive hand onto the boy's chest, pushing so hard Cap could barely breathe. The old man leaned in close.

"A pile of bones," he whispered. "That's all that will be left of you."

With that, he left. Lumbering footsteps faded away to silence.

Ignoring the aching of his head, Cap began to rock his body side to side, trying to roll himself off the table. His head felt as if it would explode with pain each time he moved it. The burlap sack over his head smelled of rotting produce. Bile rose in his throat.

"I suggest you hold still," someone said.

Cap froze at the sound of Dr. Ivins's voice.

"You must have quite a headache, young man. You struck your head as you fell yesterday." Inches away from Cap's ears was the soft rustle of cloth, then the clink of glass bottles and the *ping* of metal striking against metal.

Cap tried to speak, but all that came out was a wet-sounding croak. He stopped moving and waited for the pounding in his head to subside.

"My friend was distressed when she saw you. I explained to her that you were responsible for kidnapping her daughter."

"No!" Cap managed to say.

"I promised to take you to the hospital and call the sheriff. Once you awoke, he would find out where you took that helpless young girl," Dr. Ivins continued in a smooth voice.

The sack was whisked from Cap's head. He blinked and stared into red-rimmed eyes, glinting inches from his own.

"Sadly, you escaped the hospital and the town is in an uproar, searching for the poor lost girl and the evil boy who took her. That boy is a member of the gang of body snatchers. Newsboys all over town are calling out your name. Of course, I told the sheriff everything. He saw fit to call on your parents."

Dr. Ivins leaned even closer. "This was a great blow to your mother. I'm afraid the shock might even cause the pains of childbirth to begin too early. You are a selfish boy, Cap," the doctor hissed into the boy's face. "A very selfish boy."

"Why are you doing this?" Cap whispered.

The man straightened and whirled around. "Dr. Rusch and I have a successful business. We ship bodies to medical schools around the country. It's easier for them to buy from us than to procure their own. They pay gladly, no questions asked."

"All those barrels," Cap said. "There are so many. Where'd they all come from?"

"Rusch and I had agreements with many of our dying patients," Dr. Ivins said in a soft voice. "Families who were reluctant to let us have the bodies of their loved ones were offered a nice sum. What we pay is nothing short of a king's ransom for most around here. With what we earned from our business, we felt we could afford to offer it."

"The arrangement," Cap said, straining against the tight ropes that held him.

Dr. Ivins nodded.

"But why did you have us dig some people up? Didn't their families want the money, too?"

Dr. Ivins sighed and closed his eyes, pinching the bridge of his nose for a moment. "We *do* pay a pretty penny, Cap," he said. "Rusch always said we should save money when we could. I hate to agree with him, but it's good business sense. Any time we can procure bodies for free, well…" he let his voice trail away.

So, they have Lum dig up the ones nobody cares about, Cap thought, wincing at the bitterness of the words. Nellie, Mr. Greeves, Mr. Jefferson…Jessamyn. *That poor old Mr. Johnson probably didn't get any money, either.*

Dr. Ivins straightened his wig. "Our business flourished, but Abe got greedy. Some of our patients weren't dying fast enough to keep up with our demand."

"What do you mean, greedy?" Cap asked. He had to keep the man talking. Surely someone would come to help.

"Oh," Dr. Ivins said, turning around, "some patients took their sweet time to die, so Abe sped things up. I didn't mind, but I found it necessary to spread the rumor of a 'strange illness,' to explain the deaths," he said. He winked at Cap like the two shared a joke. "With Abe out of the way I'll declare that I've found a cure. No need to alarm the town indefinitely."

When Cap did not respond, Dr. Ivins shrugged and began an ambling walk. "As Abe grew older and more soaked in his drink, he grew careless as well. Sometimes," the doctor added, "the dose of laudanum he administered was only enough to put his patients into a deep sleep, not kill them."

A pang struck Cap's heart. He closed his eyes. He'd already discovered that the power he thought was passed on to him did not work on everyone. But still, somewhere in the back of his mind had been the tiniest shred of hope that the power was yet there, lying in wait for the right person, the right situation.

It wasn't me who brought those people back. It was never me. I have no gift.

A wave of despair, deep as an angry ocean, engulfed him. Cap scowled at the doctor. How could the man have fooled so many people? The entire town respected him. Delphia practically worshipped him.

"Please, let me go!" Cap shouted, struggling.

"I am sorry, young man," Dr. Ivins said, smiling down at him with a kindly expression. "I hate to lose my bright young inventor, but, well..." he ruffled Cap's hair, "one must do what one must do."

Dr. Ivins placed a wooden box onto the table beside Cap's head. He unwound long wires and set what looked like metal-studded dog collars onto the boy's chest. Cap gasped.

"I see you recognize my resurrection machine," Dr. Ivins said with pride. "If money wasn't persuasive enough, at times this pretty little device did the trick." He slid one of the collars under the boy's neck.

"Families were thrilled to learn how their dear loved ones might be able to return to them. I admit that my machine has not yet worked, though I've tried it many times." He buckled the collar and cinched it tight. Cap strained to breathe. Dr. Ivins then buckled a larger collar about the boy's forehead, shoving it down, hard.

"I saw something similar long ago, in Scotland. A man was executed by hanging, but was revived for a few seconds by an electric shock. That was a sight I'll never forget. I determined that moment to study medicine so I might discover the greatest secret of all—the secret to immortality."

The doctor untied one of Cap's aching hands. He forced the metal cylinder into the boy's fist and then bound it tightly back in place. Then Dr. Ivins grasped the crank of his resurrection machine and smiled. "I must thank you, Cap. Before he passed, Mr. Garrett told me it was your idea to put more magnets inside. It does make a much stronger current. I do regret losing the man to our mysterious illness, but, well, my machine is perfect now and I no longer require his services."

Cap blinked in horror, but the next moment, he screamed as a tingling jolt shot through his body. Heat burned his forehead and neck where the collars were attached. Dr. Ivins stopped turning the crank and wiped his sweating forehead. "I need information from you, boy."

"I don't know anything," Cap said through clenched teeth. His body ached almost as much as his heart.

Dr. Ivins turned the crank again, and another jolt shot hot needles through the boy's quivering frame.

"Where is Jessamyn?" Dr. Ivins said, leaning down to snarl into the boy's face. "Tell me now."

Convulsing with tremors from head to toe, Cap could only shake his head. Dr. Ivins turned the handle faster and faster. Hot knives sliced through Cap as the jolts came in quick succession, one after another.

Finally, it stopped. But the doctor was not about to allow him any moment of rest. A rough hand slapped Cap's face, and he groaned in pain.

He opened his eyes to find a gleam of metal inches from his nose. The tiny knife glinted in the lantern light.

"I must find her," Dr. Ivins said, tapping the knife on Cap's nose. "I put you in cold storage last night so you'd have time to reflect. And you did, didn't you? You don't want to return to the grave to wait for a slow death. Well," he added, his eyes fixed on the boy's horrified face. "Do you?"

"No." Cap groaned.

"Now then," Dr. Ivins said with a grin, "if you tell me, all shall be forgiven. No more shocks. No fear of being buried alive."

"You'll let me go?" Cap whispered.

"Oh, no, young man, I never said that. What I mean is you will not be buried...*alive*."

He moved closer and Cap couldn't breathe.

"I'll make it quick if you tell me where she is," the doctor whispered into his face.

"But why do you want to kill Jessamyn?" Cap asked in a shivering voice.

"*Kill* her?" Dr. Ivins asked. He stood back. "I don't want to kill her, boy! I'm *saving* her," he said, walking slowly around the table. His eyes were distant. "Imagine my distress to hear Abe had administered his special concoction to the girl. That fool! Some schools were asking for the bodies of children, and Abe was anxious to fulfill their wishes. He thought no one would miss an orphan."

"Except for her mother," Cap whispered. "And plenty of others."

Dr. Ivins waved Cap's comment away like it was an annoying fly. "I was away at the time and only returned after her burial. I was heartbroken. I hurried to the cemetery to make certain Lum got her out of the ground quickly so I could try my machine. Of course, we both know I didn't need it after all, did I?"

"But why do you care so much about *her*?" Cap asked again.

"You ask me why I care about my own *daughter*?" Dr. Ivins spluttered.

"You're mad as anything!" Cap said. "She's not your child."

Dr. Ivins ignored him. He turned to pace the stone floor. "I can give her all that she needs," he said. "A home, an education, fine clothes, a carriage. She'll go to balls and parties, be a grand lady!"

The doctor bowed as if to an invisible dance partner, and began to waltz slowly about the room, humming. "Dance with your papa, Annalise. You look lovely, sweetheart. And so light on your feet."

"Jessamyn's *not* your daughter!" Cap said. "I saw the portrait in your office. Your daughter is dead."

For a moment, Dr. Ivins stood still where he was, his face in shadow. The stiffness of his shoulders began to relax, and his head bowed. Cap held his breath, hardly daring to hope that his words had broken through to the man's befuddled mind.

Then, Dr. Ivins shook his head, squared his shoulders, and marched to Cap. He held up the knife. "Where is she?" he whispered. "Where is my Annalise?"

Mustering all his strength, Cap bent his knees and shifted himself sideways at the same moment, so that when he kicked, his feet contacted solidly with the doctor's chest. Dr. Ivins flew backward and fell onto his little instrument-covered table, which collapsed under the man's weight. The doctor screamed and cursed, thrashing about like a fish upon the riverbank. But in moments, he grew silent.

THIRTY-THREE

C AP ROLLED HIMSELF off the table and fell to the hard floor. Groaning, he forced himself to his feet and hopped through the doorway and into the dark corridor, dragging the cursed electric box behind him.

A rapid pounding grew louder and louder as running feet drew near. The glow of a lantern appeared. Cap howled in frustration as hands seized him.

"No! Let me go!" he screamed.

"He's here, Mr. Cooper!" a deep voice shouted. Strong hands held Cap tight. A round, ugly face peered down at him. It was Sister Mariah.

"Thank God, we found him," Father said, panting. He plucked uselessly at the ropes that bound the boy's body, but managed to swiftly unbuckle the leather collar from about his neck. Cap took in great gulps of air.

Skirts rustled as Sister Mariah hurried into the dissection room but returned within moments. "Dr. Ivins has fainted," she announced. "Here, I'll cut those ropes."

Cap twisted his head around and spied the doctor's tiny knife in her hands.

"No!" he screamed. "She's with Dr. Ivins! She like as not helped him bury me. Don't let her touch me!"

"What?" Father said, pulling Cap away from Sister Mariah. "Stay away, woman!"

Sister Mariah gaped at him. The knife fell from her fingers and pinged onto the stone floor. She held a hand to her mouth.

"I would never hurt him." She breathed. Turning her eyes to Cap, she added: "Dr. Ivins *buried* you?"

"I fell and struck my head and woke up all trussed up and buried in a box. I don't know how long I was there before Lum dug me up and brought me here."

"Stay away," Father said to the now weeping woman. He seized the knife she'd dropped and sawed through the ropes that bound his son.

"How did you find me?" Cap said, wincing at the pins and needles that flooded his numb limbs.

"*She* led me here," Father said, nodding in Sister Mariah's direction. His jaw was set in a hard line. "Was this simply a trap? Is someone waiting to tie me up as well?"

"No, Mr. Cooper," Sister Mariah blubbered. "I had no idea what Dr. Ivins had done. He said he'd take Cap to the hospital. I went to find the boy and learned he'd never been there, so I came to fetch you."

Breathing in deeply, Father glowered at the woman, but then his face softened a fraction.

"That much is true," he said. "She arrived moments after the sheriff left. He told us you were seen leaving town with a girl. Your mamma and I were frantic."

"You said you had to keep me silent," Cap said, glaring at Sister Mariah. "I heard you."

"I thought he'd *pay* you," Sister Mariah sobbed. "I never meant for any harm to come to you!"

"That will be for the sheriff to decide," Father said.

Sister Mariah sank to her knees and buried her face in her hands.

"Come, son," Father said. But Cap didn't move. Rubbing his sore arms to get some feeling back, he looked the man squarely in the face.

"Why did you allow Lum to say those things about me?" he asked. "And treat me so?"

Father ran a hand through his wild hair and briefly closed his eyes.

"I was wrong, Cap. About so much. I wanted money so badly I did things I'll always regret. I hurt good people and nearly lost my only son. And nothing could ever make up for that."

Something warm sparked and spread inside Cap's chest at the bittersweet sound of those words. The part of his heart he swore had frozen solid began to thaw.

"No more working for Lum?" Cap asked.

"No more," Father promised him. He put an arm about Cap and the two moved as quickly as they could to escape the terror-filled building. Cap vowed he'd even welcome a dose of Mrs. Hardy's foul-tasting fever cure, if she thought he needed it.

As they reached the main floor, shouts and loud voices reached their ears. Then, someone began to pound on the wide front doors.

"It's the law, I hope," Father said. He reached out, but the doors burst open before he could seize the knob.

Blinded by the sudden flare of sunlight in his face, Cap held his arm over his eyes.

"It's the Cooper boy!" someone shouted. "One of the devilish body snatchers!"

Cap dropped his arm and squinted at the scene before him. The courtyard was filled with shouting people. Folks of all colors and stations mingled together, all with lowered brows and thunderous expressions. Lettie Garrett stood nearby with red-rimmed eyes, her pink cheeks streaked with tears.

Unable to meet her gaze, Cap searched the gathering for anyone possessed of a friendlier aspect. There were quite a few people he knew: the grocer, the librarian, Master Rankin, and some boys from school, including Eli. Cap even spied the round woman who'd listened in on his talk with Jessamyn. But they all gawked at Cap and Father like they were oddities on display inside a carnival tent.

"You two come on out," a broad, gray-bearded man told them in a gruff voice. He motioned Cap and Father outside. Two other men, one a dark-skinned man dressed in shirt sleeves and the other a short, pale man wearing a spattered butcher's apron, stood in front of them with folded arms. The two hovered so close Cap had no doubt they meant to keep him and Father from fleeing.

"Let's go inside and find our dead!" the bearded man shouted. A stream of people pushed their way inside the Round House.

Those who remained outside muttered among themselves, while casting angry glances at the boy and his father. A few faces were twisted with fury, and Cap took a step backward until he was stopped by the brick wall of the medical college.

"Now, everybody, stay calm," a deep voice said. The towering man Cap had seen with Jardine and Delphia moved through the crowd. His face was grim. "I don't know Mr. Cooper, but my wife and daughter say his family is kind and honorable," he said. "Let's give the two a chance to explain all this."

"You said it, Reverend," the round woman said, elbowing her way forward. "I heard that child talk to someone the other day, and he was right decent. I want to hear what he has to say now." She rewarded Cap with a steady gaze that at least wasn't accusatory.

"You go on home, Sally," the brown-skinned man who stood watch told her.

Sally put her hands on her hips. "You going to make me?" Someone in the crowd chuckled.

Father put an arm around his son. He was trembling. Then Mr. Jackson stepped away from the throng in the courtyard, while loud whispers filled the air. He clutched his hat in his hands.

"Where's my Nellie?" he said. "I only want to know where she is. That's all I'm asking." His eyes pleaded.

Cap opened his mouth, but his words seemed to have lodged themselves somewhere deep in his chest.

"And where's my papa?" Lettie stepped forward until she stood beside Mr. Jackson. "I opened his coffin after the wake to give him his favorite watch. Nothing was there. That box was empty!" The girl burst into tears, and Mr. Jackson handed her a handkerchief, which she accepted with a nod.

Reverend Cole spoke quietly to Father. "Will you answer their questions, sir?"

Father grew pale. "I can't. Please," he added, raising his voice, "let me explain why we're here. I was searching for my son. You all know he was missing."

The whispers swelled like a rising windstorm. A woman called: "He was missing because he took that poor girl, that's why!"

"Please, let me speak," Father said, holding his hands out. Reverend Cole motioned for silence. "I knew my son didn't leave town and had reason to believe he might be here. He was. All tied up and nearly dead, to boot."

"The papers say he was one of *them*," a man shouted. "He's one of those ghouls stealing our dead. And I'll be blamed if you ain't one o' them, too."

Father clamped his lips closed.

"You were his friend," Lettie said, sniffling. She looked Cap in the eye. "How could you?"

"But I didn't," Cap said, while his heart thrummed furiously. "I didn't even know he was dead." He wiped his sweaty palms on his trousers.

"Are you saying you folks didn't take my Nellie?" Mr. Jackson asked. He gripped his hat so tightly it was nearly crushed against his chest.

Unable to answer, Cap gulped, glancing at Father for help. But Father hesitated, flicking his eyes toward the men who stood guard. Voices rose around them until the sound was like the roar of a debris-choked river after a storm.

There was a sudden ripple in the crowd, giving the mass of bodies the appearance of an undulating sea. Tillie and Jessamyn pushed their way through until they reached the front. The girl's braid had come undone and her hair waved wildly about her face.

At the sight, Cap's insides trembled. After what she'd witnessed at Delphia's house, how could Jessamyn see him as anything but a monster?

"We want to know the truth," Tillie called in a ragged voice. "What happened to my daughter? And Jardine's poor little baby? I know you had him. Jessie told me."

Sally cocked her head to one side as she regarded Cap with narrowed eyes. The boy ducked his head.

"What happened to Nellie?" Mr. Jackson yelled. "Somebody's got to come clean some time, and I ain't going to shut my mouth until I hear the truth."

With bowed shoulders, Cap took a deep breath. There was no way to hide the truth any longer. He allowed himself a final yearning look at Jessamyn's face. Unshed tears sparkled in her eyes.

"We did dig some people from their graves," Cap called. He glanced at Father, who rewarded him with a slight nod. "But we didn't dig up everybody. Some people had an arrangement. The doctors paid to take them away after they died."

Gasps of surprise and horror erupted around them. Lettie clapped a hand over her mouth.

Reverend Cole flew to stand directly in front of Cap. "Who paid them? Which doctors? Tell me, son. Please."

Before Cap could answer, men poured out of the Round House and surrounded them.

"We found bodies!" one shouted. "The place is plumb filled with 'em, and they've killed one of the doctors!"

Cap took a breath to speak, but his air was suddenly cut off. A strong arm wrapped itself around his neck and he was dragged backward. Blood pounded in his ears, but he still heard the shrill sound of Jessamyn's screams as the world began to turn dark.

THIRTY-FOUR

H IS ATTACKER RELEASED his neck but seized him by the hair. Cap gulped for air and struggled to keep his footing.

"Give me my daughter, or I'll kill him!" Dr. Ivins said in an icy voice. He held up a razor-sharp knife as his pale eyes searched the crowd, falling upon Jessamyn. "There she is!" he cried, pointing with the blade. The girl screamed and shrank back.

"Dr. Ivins? Is that you?" Reverend Cole cried.

The doctor turned his gaze to the man. His bald head shone in the winter sunlight and his face was contorted. "I am here for my daughter. This boy has stolen her, and I want her back."

"Doc, what are you doing?" Father shouted.

"Give me my daughter!" screamed Dr. Ivins. He shook Cap and lowered the knife.

"She's *not* your daughter!" Tillie shouted. She pushed Jessamyn behind her. "Her father was Josiah Henson, my husband. He was a former slave from Kentucky."

"From Madison?" Sally squealed. "The son of Billy and Abigail?" Tillie nodded, her face a mask of shock.

Sally threw her arms in the air as though she were at a church revival and shouted: "Lord be praised! Josiah was my own sister's child!" Without another word, the woman rushed to stand beside Tillie and Jessamyn. "You ain't going to touch that girl," she said, planting her hands on her hips. "She's my family."

Dr. Ivins raised his knife. More than one person screamed. Cap squeezed his eyes shut, but the stinging cut he expected never came. Instead, a *clang* and a *thud* sounded in his ears, and Dr. Ivins let go.

Cap dropped, gasping for air. The doctor lay upon the ground with blood dripping into his closed eyes. Sister Mariah stood over him, still holding aloft a metal bedpan. She dropped it to the earth and leaned against the side of the building, breathing hard.

"What's all this?" Sheriff Isaccson shouted. "Move aside and let me through!" The hard-faced man and several deputies shoved through the small knot of people until they stood before Cap and his father.

So many people began to talk at once, yelling and pointing, that the sheriff fired his pistol into the air. The thick silence that followed was broken only by the sound of a dog barking furiously.

"I will give everyone a chance to speak," the man said drily, replacing his pistol in its holder, "but for now, I'd like to speak to the Coopers. Maybe the rest of you all could go on home."

"This is my fault, Sheriff," Sister Mariah said. "I'm afraid there's nasty business afoot, and I am to blame, not those two." She squared her shoulders. "Let this man and his son go, and I'll explain it all."

"They'll stay right where they are," the sheriff said. The stocky man ordered his deputies to fetch a stretcher for Dr. Ivins. After the man was carried off to the hospital, the sheriff motioned for Cap and his father to sit on the steps.

Some of the onlookers finally left at the sheriff's orders. Tillie hurried her daughter away, while Sally bustled after the two, firing fast questions at them. She begged them to come to her home to get warm and have tea. Tillie accepted with a tremulous smile. Jessamyn gave Cap a tiny wave, though she didn't smile. Cap did his best to convince himself that she would speak to him again. Maybe someday.

Revered Cole took Wilford Jackson by the arm and led the man to a nearby worker's cart. They sat and turned weary faces toward the lawmen. Lettie hovered near them, clutching her coat tightly about her neck.

"Sheriff, you may want to ask them about an arrangement to take bodies in exchange for pay. The boy mentioned it," Reverend Cole said.

"Nobody offered me money for my Nellie," Mr. Jackson said. He put his crushed hat on his head. "But I never woulda taken it, nohow."

The sheriff began to question Sister Mariah, who insisted Cap and his father had nothing to do with the dead stored inside the college.

"Medical schools need bodies," she said in a quiet voice. "And they'll pay handsomely for them."

"And that arrangement? What was the Reverend talking about?"

In a shaking voice, the woman explained.

"You paid folks so those two could dig up their bodies? Seems like a real bother to me to make those fellows do such hard work," the sheriff said.

"You don't understand," Sister Mariah said. She cast a worried glance over at the Reverend and Mr. Jackson, and her shoulders slumped. "They paid the people who, uh…"

"They paid the people who had families that…well, that the law would have listened to," Cap said. The more he thought of the wretched business he'd been involved in, the worse he felt. He ducked his head and ran a hand through his wild curls. "The ones nobody would really care about, well, they had us dig them up. That way, they wouldn't have to pay. Dr. Ivins said so himself."

Reverend Cole rubbed his hand over his face. Mr. Jackson shook his head slowly. Lettie closed her eyes.

"They must have paid my father," she said. "I wondered where Papa got the money he left me, and now I know. Oh, Papa," she said, pressing her hand to her lips.

"Now, how in tarnation could a God-fearing woman such as yourself get involved in all this?" the sheriff asked Sister Mariah.

The woman hung her head. "It was for the children," she said in a trembling voice. "It was always for them. I didn't know how else I'd keep my doors open and feed my orphans."

The sheriff's eyes narrowed but he didn't reply. Instead, he turned toward Father.

"And what about you, Mr. Cooper. How did you get yourself tangled in this?" he asked.

Father closed his eyes and sighed. "I had to pay for medicine and doctors," he said in a quiet voice. "My wife..." his shoulders sagged and his voice trailed off.

"I'll swear on the Bible they only helped dig up bodies. They didn't know about the business of shipping bodies out of state," Sister Mariah said.

"The *what?*" the sheriff said. Just then, a deputy hurried outside.

"There are thirteen bodies in barrels," he said, wrinkling his nose. "I've never seen anything like it."

"I'm afraid you'll find more in town," Sister Mariah said. "I'll tell you where they are."

The lawman's face turned to stone. Slowly, he shook his head. "Is that all?" he asked in a steely voice.

"No," Cap blurted. "It's not all. Dr. Rusch was killing folks with too much medicine, then saying they'd died from the new illness. That's how come they got so many bodies."

The few who remained in the courtyard exclaimed in horror.

"I didn't know," Sister Mariah said. She began to sob. "Please believe me! I had no idea that was happening!"

The sheriff turned to Sister Mariah. "I reckon we'll let the courts decide what you knew."

"And you," the lawman said, turning toward Father. "How could you involve your boy in something like this?"

Father didn't raise his head. With a huff, the sheriff spoke to him in a low voice. "I'll let you take him home for now. But don't you leave town."

Father nodded, and the sheriff led Sister Mariah away.

Cap and Father finally headed home. When they reached their front door, the boy hung back. "What's Mamma going to say to us?" he whispered.

Father shook his head. "I guess we're about to find out," he said.

T HE MAN NAMED Parsons awoke with a pounding headache and a thirst that an ocean full of drink couldn't quench.

It was hot. Parsons pulled his sweat-soaked shirt away from his damp skin. He hadn't lit a fire. He was out of coal. The man yawned, drew in a deep breath, and his crinkled face took on a sour grimace. His closet-like room at the back of the boarding house stank like the trash heaps of hell.

He rose from the chair where he'd slept off his drink and shuffled to the bed. He'd allowed his friend, Lum Jones, to take the single bed. Land o' Goshen, his head ached and that smell was unholy.

Parsons blinked and shuffled on trembling legs, sniffing the air and nearly choking. A heavy gray haze filled the room. The smoke was acrid and fetid, smelling of burnt hair and what reminded Parsons of cooked meat.

"Lum?" Parsons choked out, "you awake?"

Lum didn't answer. Parsons raised the brown paper blind as he passed the window, allowing winter sunlight to stream in.

Smoke curls rose lazily in the air and hovered above the bed, where they danced in the sunshine. The charred edges of blanket and mattress surrounded an oblong hole that extended from headboard to footboard. Somehow, flames had burned hot, eating right through the center of the mattress, exposing, but not singeing, the wooden slats beneath. What was left of the bed's former occupant was nothing but a pile of ashes, greasy and gray and stinking. The dark ashes covered the slats of the bed frame and lay piled on the floor.

Parsons moaned, seized his coat, and fled. He wasn't about to be blamed for this.

THIRTY-FIVE

"OH, THANK YOU, dear Lord," Mrs. Hardy said when the two opened the door. Her hands fluttered to her face as she regarded the boy. "Cap, Mina has been frantic! Where were you?" She flew to his side and wrapped him in a tearful embrace.

"Later," Father said. "We must speak to Mina."

"She's abed," Mrs. Hardy said, wringing her apron with her hands. Tears spilled over as she spoke. "And feverish with worry. Oh, do hurry! She must be told that Cap is all right."

The woman shooed them up the stairs. "I'll bring chamomile tea. I sent a neighbor for the doctor, but she couldn't find him. She said there was an uproar in town." Mrs. Hardy hurried back down the hall, making the sign of the cross as she walked. "But you're back. Oh, praise be!"

Father tapped on Mamma's door. She called in her soft voice: "Mrs. Hardy? Have you heard anything?"

"He's safe, Mina," Father said in a trembling voice. He opened the door. "Cap is home."

Mamma's face crumpled at the sight of her son. Mutely, she held out her arms, and Cap ran to her embrace.

"I was so frightened," she sobbed, stroking his hair. "Oh, Cap."

When Mamma's sobs turned into quiet trembling, Cap sat back and drew his handkerchief from his pocket. He handed it to his mother, who dabbed her streaming eyes.

"We must let you rest," Father said.

"Wait," Mamma said, reaching to put a hand on her son's arm. "I want to know what happened."

"Please, Mina," Father said. He ran a hand through his already wild hair. "We'll tell you later."

Though her cheeks were crimson with fever and damp with tears, Mamma sat up and looked directly into her husband's eyes. "I'm not a hothouse flower that will wilt and die, Noah. You'll tell me, now," she said. Snuffling, she reached under her pillow and withdrew a folded newspaper. "After what I've been reading, I believe my boys have quite a story to tell."

Father opened and closed his mouth. He glanced at Cap, and the boy rushed to speak.

"Please don't be angry with Father," he said. "He needed money to pay Doctor Ivins."

Mamma's eyes widened.

"Cap—" Father said.

"We only helped dig up bodies," Cap said. "We didn't know about that business the doctors had, shipping bodies to medical schools. Sister Mariah was in on it. And Lum."

Mamma's jaw dropped. The newspaper fell to the floor.

"Cap," Father said. "Hush!"

"Go on," Mamma said. Her eyes snapped and her mouth tightened into a thin line.

Cap rushed through his tale, only pausing every so often for breath. Father paced while the boy spoke. He scowled at the floor.

Mamma's face reflected shock and horror. More than once, she held her hands over her mouth. Finally, her wan features stilled into a mask of deep sadness. When Cap paused for breath, Mamma silenced him with a wave of her hand.

"Noah," she said softly. Mutely, she reached out.

Father knelt at the side of the bed and took his wife's hand.

"I'm so sorry," he said. His shoulders shook.

Mamma stroked his hair while she studied his face. Her eyes glittered.

"My boys," she whispered. "How could you have..." she stopped and gulped. "How could you..." She closed her eyes.

Mrs. Hardy tapped on the door and came in, bringing a pot of tea.

"Shoo, gentlemen," she said to Cap and Father. "Let Mina rest, now. Oh, great heavens, I'm so glad you're all right, Cap." She set her tray down and gave the boy another swift hug.

"So am I," Mamma said, flinging aside her coverlet. "Help me up, Noah."

In mute surprise, Father took her hand and helped her to her feet. At her orders, he then found her robe and slippers.

"I've spent far too much time shut up in here," Mamma said, knotting the robe about her swollen belly. Swiftly, she dashed at her wet cheeks. "I believe I'll take my tea in the kitchen. With my family."

While Mrs. Hardy fussed and argued, Mamma took Father's arm. Still silent, he helped her downstairs. The man was so shocked he didn't say a word until they reached the front hall.

"Mina," Father said, rubbing his hand over his hair, but Mamma shushed him.

"When I'm well again, you and Cap will accompany me to church," she said. "We might raise some eyebrows, but it will do us good."

"Mina, no," Father said with a frown. "What church would want us there?"

Mamma gave him a hard look and he remained quiet. "Cap," she said, pinning her son in her gaze, "I have a book for you to read. You'll recite from it during my next literary meeting. That is, if any of the ladies will set foot in our house again."

"But, Mamma," Cap said, while Father said: "Now, Mina—"

"*Hush!*"

"Yes, ma'am," Father and Cap said at the same time.

"Mrs. Hardy?" Mamma said. "My boys have something to say to you, too."

For the next several days, Mrs. Hardy stayed away. When Cap asked Father where she was, the man only shrugged. "I don't know if she'll be back, Cap," he said, softly.

The quiet of the house was uncanny, without the Irish woman's constant chatter and off-key humming.

Told he could remain away from school until after Christmas, Cap quietly tinkered in his workshop. Father brought the morning newspapers inside along with the milk. He left them open on the kitchen table. Cap only read the headlines.

Circleville College of Medicine Now Deceased. Gang of Ghouls Gone, Cemeteries Safe at Present. Orphan Girl Returned Safe and Sound. Sheriff Investigates Death of Deadly Doctors. Local Nun Arrested for Resurrection Scheme. And Cap's favorite: *Body Snatcher Burns to Death in Boarding House: God's Vengeance or the Devil's Drink?*

Sheriff Isaccson visited several times. Cap and Father were each required to tell their tales, while a young clerk with a frowning face scribbled on a paper. Cap worried, but Father was not taken to jail.

"That nun sure did you a favor," the sheriff told Father. "She signed a statement saying you didn't do anything besides help her brother dig up graves. But she's going to trial in Columbus for her part in all this. Especially since Dr. Ivins died after she struck his head."

The morning of the fourth day after the dreadful scene at the college, Cap awoke to the smell of frying bacon and found Mrs. Hardy in the kitchen, bustling about as usual. Graying strands of hair escaped from the bun at the nape of her neck, and her starched apron was dotted with spots of porridge.

"Well, are you going to stand there, staring?" she asked him. "Sit. Eat."

Cap crossed the room and threw his arms around her. After stiffening for a moment, the woman returned his embrace and laid her cheek on his head. "Well, now," she said, sniffling. "How could I ever leave my boy?"

Late that night, Cap woke to the patter of winter rain on his window and the murmur of low voices outside his bedroom door. The knob rattled. He kept his eyes shut and tried to breathe evenly.

The door squeaked softly open and then closed again. Cap sighed in relief. He was in no mood for visitors. He *was* curious, though. Who was that? He crept to the door and put his ear to the keyhole.

"I won't wake him now," Jardine was saying. "He's young and should be fine. I like to die when I think of what that wicked man did to him."

A single thought thundered through Cap's brain. He owed Jardine an explanation. And an apology. Bolting to his feet, he flung open the door before he could lose his courage. "Wait," he blurted.

His face burned. The woman hadn't been talking to Father, or Mrs. Hardy. She had been talking to Delphia. When Cap met her gaze, the girl's eyes narrowed and her brows met in the middle.

"You'd best lie back down, Cap," Jardine said quietly. Her face was unreadable. "You must be plumb tired."

"Why, of course he's tired, Mamma," Delphia said. "He was likely up all night digging up some other poor soul."

"Delphia," Jardine said. "That awful business is ended."

"When I think of what he and those horrible men were doing, oh, it makes me so mad I could spit." The girl threw her hands in the air. "And to think I admired Dr. Ivins so. He took us all for fools, didn't he?"

"Delphia," Jardine said, "he's dead, now, and the Lord will judge."

The girl ignored her. "Land sakes, why did I agree to come to this house, Mamma? I do not want to see this boy ever again. Not after what he did to us. You hear me, Cap?" she said. Her face was a mask of pain. Tears glittered in her eyes.

Cap struggled for the right words, but there weren't any. There was only the truth.

"Please, listen! I did some bad things, but I never took your baby. I was trying to bring him back to you," he said in a rush. "I swear it, ma'am! On God and all His holy angels."

Cap swallowed as Jardine took his face in her warm, calloused hands. She stared hard into his eyes, her expression searching and full of pain. He tried to return her gaze, but found that he couldn't. Her face blurred before his eyes. He hung his head in defeat.

"I believe you," Jardine whispered. Cap raised his head.

"Mamma?" Delphia blurted. "How can you—"

"*Think*, Philadelphia," Jardine said. "I was so shocked I never stopped to think clear until now. Cap wouldn't have brought our little one to our very own home unless he meant to return him to us."

Unable to speak, Cap nodded. Then, he was enfolded in a warm embrace full of such sweetness that he knew he'd been forgiven.

"I'm so sorry," he whispered.

"So am I," Father spoke from the top of the stairs.

Straightening, Jardine turned. "Mr. Cooper?"

"I allowed Lum to take your child in the first place. I should have never done so. I was afraid Lum wouldn't give me any more work, and I wanted that money more than anything. I thought it was the only way to get enough money to help Mina. I am sorry, Mrs. Cole." Father stared in misery at the floor, his forehead crinkled and his eyes dark with emotion.

Jardine squared her shoulders. "I cannot say that I blame you for seeking the means to pay for doctors who could help your wife," she said. "But surely you must see what sadness you brought upon others."

Father nodded.

"That's why I aim to find ways for medical schools to get their bodies legally," Delphia said, pressing her lips together. "I'll do it, I swear."

"Are you still going to be a doctor?" Cap asked her.

Delphia regarded him for a long moment with a serious expression. "You try and stop me," she finally said. Her lips twitched, and she rewarded the boy with the tiniest of smiles.

With that, she turned and swept past Father and down the stairs. With a nod to the two, Jardine followed her daughter.

Father cleared his throat. "Son?" he said, placing an arm around the boy's shoulders.

"Yes?" Cap answered. Father's expression was blank. Rain spattered and wind howled around the eaves. Finally, Father's mouth started to work. His lips trembled.

"Don't let Mrs. Hardy know you were out socializing with the ladies wearing naught but your night shirt."

THIRTY-SIX

FEBRUARY 19, 1876

C AP WOKE UP early for a Saturday. He pulled on his clothes and hurried to his workshop to finish the new warming box he was making for Sally Taylor's chickens. The woman was busy building up her egg business and offered to pay him after she heard about the first box he'd made. Jessamyn and Tillie now boarded with their newly discovered relative. Tillie took in sewing and helped Sally. Jessamyn seemed much happier than she'd ever been at the orphanage.

She was still speaking to Cap.

Father knocked on the door frame as he entered. "Thought I'd see what our inventor was up to," he said. He pulled at the torn sheet covering a bulky object on the table. "Are you ever going to show me what this is, or must I come in on the sly?"

Smiling, Cap said: "I suppose you can see it now." He whisked the sheet away. "We can test it outside when the weather is warm."

"What's it for?" Father asked, touching the circular cast iron object. "Why are those wires wrapped about that contraption at the top?"

"The wire becomes the trigger," Cap explained. Father jerked his hand back like the metal was hot as a poker taken from the fire. "Oh, there's no gunpowder inside, yet. You only add that after you bury this above the coffin." Swiftly, Cap explained his invention. "I call it a 'grave torpedo.'"

"A *torpedo*?"

"Yes, sir," Cap said, flushing. "You see, when someone tries to dig up the grave, he's blown into the next county."

"After all that ruckus about folks not wanting the bodies of their loved ones taken away, who'd want to use this to blow them up?" Father asked with a grimace.

"It doesn't work like that," Cap said. "You bury this a few feet above the coffin. The explosion is for the snatchers. The body stays safe. Least, that's my idea."

"Ah." Father breathed. A slow smile spread across his face. "So much for the family business, eh?" The man chuckled. "Of course, we gave that up a few months ago, didn't we?"

Cap nodded. "I thought we might make us a new family business, selling this invention if it works. I hear they can use them anywhere near a medical college."

Father put a hand on his son's shoulder. "You've always had a quick mind, Cap. I'm proud of you. And, by the way, a fellow at work asked me about buying one of your warming boxes. I suppose your tinkering has its uses."

Cap ducked his head and smiled.

"You hear about Sister Mariah?" Father asked suddenly.

"Yes, sir," the boy said. He returned to his worktable. "I read the papers."

Father cleared his throat. "I'm not surprised she was found innocent. She's a nun who runs an orphanage, after all. Besides that, it was those doctors who killed their patients to have more bodies. And even though Dr. Ivins died after she hit him with that bedpan, she only struck him to save you. If he'd been well, that probably wouldn't have done him in, but he was weak from losing blood." Father glanced at Cap as he spoke the last few words.

Squeezing his eyes shut, the boy relived the moment he'd kicked the doctor, sending him crashing onto the table covered with sharp instruments.

"It wasn't your fault, son," Father swiftly said, putting his hand on Cap's shoulder. "You did what you had to do to escape. And I'm glad you did."

Taking a deep breath, Cap spoke. "Is Sister Mariah back in town?"

"Yes. In fact, she called on us yesterday while you were at school," Father replied. "To see Mina and say she was sorry for her hand in our family's troubles."

"What did Mamma say to her?" Cap asked, blinking.

Father traced a pattern in the frost on one of the window panes. "She invited Mariah to her next literary meeting."

The old clock in the corner ticked slowly.

"Well," Cap finally said. "I reckon she needs more ladies. Lots of the ones who used to come don't anymore."

Rustling filled the hallway, and Mrs. Hardy burst into the tiny room.

"The baby's coming," she said breathlessly, giving the two a stern look. "You two stay away."

Father stood and then sat again, looking wildly about the shop as though he might find something useful to do.

"Shall I fetch Jardine?" Cap asked, bolting to his feet.

"She's already here," Mrs. Hardy said over her shoulder as she hurried back to Mamma's room. "She stopped in to bring herbs for Mina."

The long day crawled by. Cap and Father remained mostly in the shop, where the boy tinkered feverishly and Father paced and bit his nails. Neither could eat. At seven o'clock, the two turned as footsteps approached the door.

"The baby's arrived," Mrs. Hardy said when she appeared. Her face drooped with fatigue.

"Mina?" Father asked, bolting to his feet.

"She's well," Mrs. Hardy answered, "but the baby..." Her voice broke.

Cap leapt to his feet and bolted down the hall, brushing past Mrs. Hardy.

No! It isn't fair!

The words tore through his brain, flowed in his veins, and pulsed through his heart. Cap burst into his mother's room.

Mamma lay in her bed with the covers pulled up to her chin. Her sweat-soaked hair was plastered to her skull. Her eyes were closed. Jardine bathed her face with a cloth and whispered softly to her as she did so. Tears slid down Mamma's cheeks.

Jardine looked up.

"Where?" He breathed.

"She's in the kitchen," the woman whispered.

The baby was lying in a basket on the table, naked atop a towel. Her skin was mottled red and white. Her eyes were closed in her tiny, round face. A thatch of hair, dark as Father's, swirled atop her head. Cap reached out to touch it. It was impossibly soft, like strands of corn silk.

He picked her up. She weighed more than Jardine's baby boy, but not by much. Tears pooled in Cap's eyes. Nearby was the basin Mrs. Hardy had prepared to bathe the baby. The heated water sent tendrils of steam into the air.

Please, God, this isn't fair, none of this. If you didn't give me a gift that would bring her back, why can't you at least tell me what to do? he prayed.

She's cold. The thought came gently to Cap, floating inside his head.

Cap moved swiftly. He placed the baby in the warm water and rubbed her tiny limbs, her stomach, her back. He trickled water over her head, washed her face clean with gentle fingers; her nose, her mouth.

"Boy, what on earth are you doing?" Jardine asked. She dropped her basket of soiled linens and hurried to his side.

Cap lifted his sister from the water. He placed the dripping baby onto the towel and swaddled her within its soft folds.

"She's cold," he said. "She has to get warm." As he spoke, his foot bumped against the very first warming box he'd fashioned for new chicks. It was still where he'd left it, shoved under the table, ready for its spring occupants. His heart leapt as an idea came to him. The chicks would have to wait.

Kneeling, Cap laid his sister inside the box and covered her with another towel. He hurriedly filled one of the thick rubber bottles with steaming water from the basin and placed it into the space below the main chamber. The metal base of the box heated up quickly. Cap added one more bottle for good measure, tucking it this time right beside the tiny infant. He ignored Jardine's fretful sounds as she watched him.

"Child," Jardine said. She knelt beside him. "I understand. I truly do. Let her go."

Cap squeezed his eyes shut and placed his hand upon his sister's tiny head.

Please.

When he opened his eyes, he saw something he didn't quite understand. Two tiny spots of pink dotted the baby's cheeks. He stroked her soft skin with a trembling finger. The sensation of warmth startled him.

He gasped.

"What is it?" Jardine asked. She leaned down and peered into the box.

The baby's eyelids fluttered. It was a slight movement, no greater than the beating of a moth's wings; the merest flicker.

And then she opened her eyes.

July 11, 1876

An advertisement appeared in the pages of the *Columbus Gazette*, the *Philadelphia Herald*, and the *New York Times*:

Cooper & Son present their invention: The Grave Torpedo. Worried that grave ghouls might disturb the peaceful rest of your dearly departed? Sow this handy gadget above the final resting place and have no fear of robbers!

"Sleep well, sweet angel; let no fears of ghouls disturb thy rest. Above thy shrouded form lies a torpedo, ready to make minced meat of anyone who attempts to convey you to the pickling vats."

HISTORICAL NOTE

Dear Reader,

In 1875, Cap's world was one of complicated social issues, much like our time. But many things were very different. People of African descent were frequently described as "colored." This word can be found often in Ohio newspaper articles from Cap's day, and I used it in order to remain true to the time period. Some other issues include the fact that people of color could not vote, and in some states, children of different races did not attend school together. American women (of all races) did not have the right to vote until 1920, and it was very unusual for any woman to consider attending medical school. Many people had fewer rights and opportunities during Cap's time, compared to what we're used to in our modern world.

Finally, body snatching really happened in the United States, even into the early part of the twentieth century. After passing laws to make it easier for schools to obtain cadavers legally (they were allowed unclaimed bodies and those of executed criminals), along with advances in refrigeration, body snatching thankfully became a thing of the past. But it was a real issue in Cap's time. Newspapers often advertised items such as "snatcher proof" cast-iron coffins and even grave torpedoes designed to foil unsuspecting robbers. In fact, an 1879 newspaper advertisement for a grave torpedo invented by Circleville resident Thomas N. Howell contains the very lines that begin with: "sleep well, sweet angel, let no fear of ghouls disturb thy rest…" which I used at the end of the story.

During this time period, inventors like Cap kept busy coming up with ideas for new products they thought would be useful. Some inventions, like incubators such as Cap's "warming box," became commonplace. Others, such as grave torpedoes, remain odd reminders of a very different time.

Rebecca Bischoff

ACKNOWLEDGMENTS

I'll never forget the experience I had at a writing conference several years ago. Every participant was given the same picture—the painting of a young fairy. We were all given time to come up with a story idea. For whatever reason, a scene popped into my head that seemed to have nothing to do with the picture. In my mind's eye, I saw a boy, maybe twelve or thirteen, digging up a grave (I wasn't even sure why). I clearly saw the boy's shocked expression when he uncovered the face of someone he recognized. I don't know how the image of a fairy sparked such an odd idea, but *The Grave Digger* came into being after that conference.

Every book is, of course, a group effort, and this story would not be the same without the support of many people. A number of friends, some who are members of my writing group, have given good advice. These include Spring Paul, Amber Buckley, Kristina Ursenbach, Gaby Thomason, and Lars Christiansen. I'm grateful to all of you for listening to my ideas. I'm especially grateful to those who took the time to read through various versions of my story and shared invaluable suggestions and feedback.

The team at Amberjack Publishing has been wonderful to work with. Rayne Stone was a patient and very perceptive editor.

Tambe provided artwork with a wonderfully spooky feel. I was thrilled to know there were others who cared as much about my story and characters as I did. I'll always be grateful to everyone who helped create this book.

ABOUT THE AUTHOR

Rebecca Bischoff lives in Southern Idaho with her family. Her debut novel, *The French Impressionist*, was published in 2016. It received an Idaho Author Award in the Young Adult category.

Rebecca loves to read everything from mysteries to paranormal to historical novels. She has a special place in her heart for stories that are a little creepy, and is fascinated by real events from history that are less well-known (and a little on the dark side). Visit her website at www.rebeccabischoffbooks.com.

ABOUT THE ILLUSTRATOR

Tambe is a children's books illustrator from Italy.

He loves to work with pen and ink on atmospheric tales of mystery and monsters, but also to spend hours in old bookshops and creepy woods. He works under the close supervision of his cat, who sometimes also takes care of replying to emails.

He recently illustrated a series of short stories by Terry Deary published by Bloomsbury UK.